Death on a Dirty Afternoon

Colin Garrow

Death on a Dirty Afternoon

© Colin Garrow 2016

ALL RIGHTS RESERVED
All rights reserved. Without limiting the rights under the copyright reserved above, no part of this publication may be reproduced, stored in, or introduced into a retrieval system, or transmitted in any form or by any means (electronic, mechanical, photocopying, recording, or otherwise) without prior written permission.

Published by Colin Garrow

ISBN-13: 978-1540587923

ISBN-10: 1540587924

Chapter 1

Frank Armstrong had lain down on the dining room table before, but in the past he'd always been either sound asleep or dead drunk. Now he was just dead.

I stared at his half-open mouth and washed-out face, and marvelled at the way his body seemed to barely inhabit the crappy suit he always wore. If I were the sort to feel guilty, I might wonder if it had been my fault, him being dead, I mean. But I wasn't.

Behind me, the blonde coughed like she needed attention.

'Why'd you call me?' I said.

'I just...' She shrugged. 'Wanted someone here, y'know? And you were his friend. I thought ye'd want to know.' She pouted at me, then seemed to remember she was supposed to be the grieving widow and turned it into a whimper.

'You call an ambulance?'

'I expect they'll send one, but what's the point? He's stone cold.' She sniffed. 'Doctor's on his way.'

Her face was conspicuously free of tears, and even though it was only eight in the morning and she'd probably only been home an hour, I could see she'd taken time to tart herself up before receiving visitors. Only the wonky hairdo and excess luggage under her eyes, showed she'd been shagging all night.

'You think it was..?' I hesitated. 'I mean..?'

'I know what ye mean, bonny lad. Ye mean was it natural causes or did I smack him over the head once too often for being a boring shit?' She sniffed again and dabbed her nose with a hanky. 'No. I expect his heart packed in. Bound to, sooner or later.'

I nodded and wondered if she realised there'd be an autopsy.

Lizzy glanced out the window and made a face. 'Tch, look at that nosy cow. I should've left the nets up.'

I turned to look. A woman across the road was standing at her front door, watching. With two pairs of eyes on her, the offender backed inside and shut the door. As we stood watching, I noticed Frank's car wasn't outside. I didn't say anything to his wife. She had enough to deal with just now.

There was a pause while Lizzy brushed unseen fluff from her blouse. She fiddled with the curtains and wiped a finger through the dust on the windowsill. I got the feeling there was something else in the pipeline.

Eventually, in an oh-I've-just-remembered sort of way, she said, 'You wouldn't be goin past Ronnie's, by any chance?'

When I looked her full in the face, she dropped her gaze to the carpet.

'Wondered if ye wouldn't mind callin at the office? Tellin the lads, an that?' She bit her lower lip the way she always did when she was pushing her luck. 'I made a couple of phone calls, ye know, family an that, but I'm not up to talking to anyone else yet.'

Of course. That's why she'd called me. Not because she felt in need of a friend, bit of moral support, which'd be fair enough, you might think. No, she wanted someone to take the crap that Frank's boss would be dishing up with a hot spoon. Or more to the point, when the brown stuff hit the proverbial and Big Ronnie went ballistic, she didn't want to be in the firing line. The fact of Frank being dead wouldn't get in the way of Ronnie taking back what was his.

'Aye, of course.' I shuffled my feet. 'I should go.'

'I was at Dave's place last night.' She showed me her 'sorry' face. 'I could tell you were wonderin, like.'

'Aye.'

She threw her hands up as if the frustration of it all was truly overwhelming. 'I mean how was I supposed to know? Never told me where he was going or nothin.'

'He was at work, wasn't he? So ye did know where he was, pretty much.'

'I knew he was drivin a bloody taxi. Course I did, but...' She ran out of steam and excuses at the same time.

Relenting a little, I allowed her a small slice of benefit-of-the-doubt pie. 'So you weren't here when he died. It wouldn't have made any difference.' I glanced at Frank. 'Not to him.' I started for the door.

'I'll let you know when the funeral is.' She

touched my hand. 'Ye'll come?'

It was only then, in that few seconds of human contact, that I felt the tears start. Not for her, mind, not that selfish, money-grabbing bitch. I looked back at the body on the table. 'I'll be there, Lizzy,' I said. And I would be - for Frank.

It was a seaside town like any other seaside town: from the non-existent sand dunes and candy-striped deck chairs to the concrete piers and tacky market stalls, we had it all. Whether you wanted to sit on the beach or prop up the nearest bar, there was something for everyone - so long as whatever you were looking for didn't amount to much. I'd like to say the tourists loved it, but they didn't, and the ones that said they did were lying.

Years ago, the place was a Mecca for gamblers, with casinos and gambling dens up and down the seafront and northern gangsters pitting their wits against the sharp suits from the south - Gateshead. I'd lived in the 'Bay' all my life, apart from twenty years in London and the odd weekend in Skegness, and I'd been around the block a few times, in both directions. So I knew the score, kind of.

I'd like to say it was My Town. But it wasn't. I just lived there.

Out in the street, I glanced back at Lizzy. She was still standing by the window looking at Frank. No wonder the neighbours were watching - not every day you see a middle-aged bloke in a suit lying dead on his own dining room table. You'd think the silly bitch would have the sense to draw the curtains, but that's Lizzy all round - let the world watch while you squeeze out the big fat turds of your life, or something along those lines.

It was spitting on to rain and I debated whether to walk back to the flat and get the car, but I'd have ended up walking the same distance anyway, so I headed up Inkerman, into Kitchener and crossed Winston Lane. I did my usual trick of nipping in the back entrance of Boots and out the other side onto the High Street by which time the rain had really got going.

Pulling my collar up, I stood for a minute in the doorway, casting about for a friendly face. Over the road there was a blue Nissan Crappy with its hazards on - not exactly a welcoming visage, but it'd do for now. I came up behind the car and jumped into the passenger seat.

'Jeezas Terry, I nearly filled me pants there.' Fat Barry flicked his cigarette out the window and shoogled round in his seat. 'Not got a job yet?'

I shook my head. 'You know I've not.'

'Oh, aye.'

His happy smiling face told me he hadn't heard the news. Given that the two of them were supposed to be great mates, I thought it best to break it to him gently. 'Frank's dead.'

He laughed, then clocking my own unlaughy face, allowed his guffaws to fade. 'You're fuckin jokin?'

'His wife thinks it was his heart.'

'Heart attack? Christ.' He let out a long sigh, generously sharing a hint of the kebab he'd had for supper the night before. He sighed again. 'Christ. When?'

'Last night by the looks of it. Lizzy came home and found him.'

'Bet she was out shaggin that Davy from the arcade, was she?' He shook his head sadly. 'Poor bugger.'

I wasn't sure if he meant Davy or Frank, but I wasn't going to ask. 'Anyway, I said I'd let Ronnie know.'

Barry's mouth dropped open again. 'You're not, though? Tellin Ronnie?'

'I said I would. Unless you want to do it?' It wasn't a serious question, but Barry thought it was.

'Like shite. He'd tear me a new ringpiece.' He gave me his serious look. 'He'd tear you a new ringpiece.' He dropped his voice. 'You know Frank owed him ten grand?'

I nodded.

'Well?'

'Well what? Not going to give it back now, is he?'

The fat man sucked in his cheeks, reminding me of that old joke about the camel and the bricks. 'He'll not be happy.' He paused, then, 'That's why you're away to tell Ronnie. Suppose ye canna expect her to do it. Not when she's just lost her husband an that. And especially not when she owes him ten big ones.' He gave me a funny look. 'She didn't ring you up to go over there just to ask you to do her dirty

work? What a bitch.'
'Hardly dirty work, Barry. Her husband just died. Ye can't blame her for that.' I felt justified saying this, cos even though I did blame her, there was no need for anyone else to do the same. Not just yet anyway.

Barry mused on the solemnity of the occasion for several minutes until I began to wonder if he'd have any eulogising left for the funeral.

'You want a lift?'

I nodded at the meter. 'You've got a fare.'

'Just a wait-and-return for Mrs Arthur and that daft cousin of hers. They'll be twenty minutes yet.'

'No, you're all right.' I slid a finger into the door handle and pulled. 'And Barry —'

'What?'

'Stay off the radio.' I winked at him and climbed out the car. It wasn't necessary to warn him off, but my fat friend had a nasty habit of dropping bombshells on behalf of others, and I didn't want to walk into the office to find I'd been pre-empted.

It took me ten minutes to walk down to the taxi office on the sea front. Nestled in-between a takeaway and a tattooist, I'd always wondered if there was something alphabetical going on when Ronnie had pooled his dubious resources and rented the place a year or two earlier, but any sense of symmetry would've been lost on the folk round here.

I pushed open the door and went upstairs.

The reception area was a wide room with a

counter across the middle and a variety of dining room chairs against the far wall. Two punters were waiting, reading month-old copies of Men's Health.

'Hello Terry, bit early for you, isn't it?' Carol's smile was the best reason for showing my face at Ron's Taxis, though the view of the bay was almost worth the trip, when it wasn't pissing down. At thirty-nine and a bit, she was only a few years younger than me, but she still managed to look amazing first thing in the morning.

'Never too early to see you, pet.'

She slid the headphones off, swivelled her chair round and scooted across the lino to the end of the counter. 'I'll put the kettle on, eh?'

I shook my head. 'No, you're all right, I'm not stoppin.' My face told her more than I'd intended and she stood up, leaning on the desk.

'What's happened? You all right?'

Nodding towards the office, I said, 'Is anyone in?' The question wasn't necessary, since I could see a blurred shape through the frosted glass.

She glanced at the punters and mouthed *You okay?*

I mouthed back that I was fine. 'Is he in?'

A voice crackled over the radio. Carol pushed a hand through her hair and moved back to the microphone. 'That you, Billy? Do 42 Eldon Street going up to Asda.'

The voice crackled in the affirmative.

She jerked her head and I moved closer. 'Ronnie's on a job,' she said, 'but the old man's in, an he's not shoutin anymore so he must be off the phone.' She waved a hand towards the wood-chipped wall that separated her and the punters from the bosses.

I poked my head around the door. Of the two desks pushed together in the middle of the tiny room, only one was occupied. Glancing at the back door, I was reassured to see it was bolted. If the younger member of the Thompson family decided to come up the back way, I'd at least get a bit of warning.

Ken didn't bother to look up. 'Oh aye? And what do you want?' It wasn't obvious from his expression if he already knew why I was there, so I hesitated, one hand on the door. I watched as he tapped one-fingeredly at his keyboard, as if he'd only recently learned how to spell.

After a moment, he raised his head and made eye contact. 'Come on then, if you're comin in.' He indicated the empty chair.

I made myself comfortable and folded my hands in my lap.

'If you're wantin your job back, ye can go fuck yourself.' There was no malice in his voice, but I knew he wasn't joking.

'Ronnie not in?'

He stopped typing. 'Why d'you want to see Ronnie?'

'I don't.'

He let out a long breath. 'Oh, like that, is it? Go on, then. Give iz the bad news.'

The flat on Otterburn Terrace wasn't anyone's idea of palatial accommodation, but the high ceilings and double-fronted windows, gave it the appearance of one of those dockside shitehouse apartments that folk with less sense than money think is the bee's bollocks.

Allowing the front door to clatter shut like a big clattery thing, I took my time climbing up to the top floor. If Sharon was still there, I didn't want to surprise her, but as it turned out, I needn't have bothered - the front door was locked and the boxes she'd piled up on the landing had gone. No hanging about for her.

Throwing the keys into the papier mâché bowl I'd made when I was ten, I stood for a while in the passage, noting the empty spaces on the coat rack and the missing CD's in the floor-to-ceiling-bookcase that was lovingly squashed into the alcove between the kitchen and living room doors. I let my gaze settle on the middle shelf and without looking too closely, I could see she'd at least left me the Bix Beiderbecke records. Nice.

I put some coffee on and spent an hour getting reacquainted with what was left of my flat. Naturally, she'd taken the lava lamps and vintage travel posters. The spaces where all her stuff had been gave the place a strange sense of insignificance, though not necessarily in a bad way. To make myself feel better, I moved the furniture round, putting it back where it had been originally, before I'd been daft enough to let Sharon loose with all that Feng Shui shite.

If this were a normal Saturday, I'd be still in bed with coffee and toast after a night picking up the dregs of the town til the early hours, but this wasn't a normal Saturday, and not just because of Frank.

I finished off the last of the so-called Mexican blend while reminding myself of the state of my bank account. I've never been good with money so wasn't used to being in anything but the red, but that'd changed a few weeks before when my sister handed over my half of what was left after we'd paid for the funeral. At a little over forty thousand, it wasn't exactly a fortune, but it'd given me the impetus to pack in driving a taxi for a living.

Even so, it would've been useful if the old bugger had died six months ago, when the money could still have made a difference, but Sharon had spent too many nights waiting up, and too many Fridays sitting in the pub on her own, clinging to a dream that eventually things might change. When they finally did, it turned out it was the old straw/camel's back thing and she'd already found somewhere else to live.

I'd've been happy to give her another chance if that sort of thing had appealed to her, however, she'd made her bed and she wanted to lie in it. It was only later I realised she's wasn't going to be lying in it by herself, so there didn't seem much point trying to persuade her otherwise.

When the clock on the mantle had rolled round to my normal getting-up time, I decided to spend the day shopping for all the items Sharon had taken that I couldn't live without.

One of the things she used to complain about was my routines - ever since I'd bumped into one of my dodgy mates on the way out somewhere, I'd got into the habit of looking out the front window before going downstairs. Normally, it wouldn't make any difference, but today was the exception - a dark, lumbering bulk slithered into my field of vision. Big Ronnie was heading my way and I wasn't in the mood for his sort of banter.

I just made the foot of the stairs when his ugly shadow slid across the half-glazed front door. I didn't bother to wait for him to press the buzzer and skipped out the back while my legs were still in working order. It wasn't that Ronnie was dangerous, but since he was here, he'd obviously heard the news of Frank's death, and I guessed he wasn't popping in to pass on his condolences.

The narrow lane that separated the back gardens of Otterburn Terrace and Flodden Road ran left and right across another two streets on either side. I headed left, which took me over Lansdowne Road and into an alley that led to the train station. If this had been tomorrow, there'd be a market on and I could lose myself for an hour, but it wasn't, so I headed onto the platform and over the bridge, hoping the railway track might have a similar effect on Ronnie to whatever it is that a river does to a pack of hounds chasing a wanted man.

Making my way back into town by the pretty

route, I did a bit of shopping and managed to replace about half the things Sharon had nicked from my kitchen. Admittedly, some of them were on the pricey side, but as she wouldn't be using them, I reasoned they'd last twice as long.

Thinking I'd give my pursuer a chance to get bored and go home, I passed a pleasant couple of hours in the South Sea Bubble, enjoying the latest 'guest' lager and sharing a plate of garlic potato wedges with a guy I was at school with. While the face was familiar, I couldn't recall his actual name, though as he didn't seem to remember mine either, it hardly mattered. Besides, it was chucking it down outside and I'd no desire to bump into Ronnie with me brandishing only wet hair and a moist demeanour.

So it was late afternoon when I got back to the flat and found the note pinned to the door. Quite what Big Ronnie was doing with a packet of drawing pins about his person, I couldn't imagine, but he'd put one in each corner of the A4 sheet to make sure his message didn't go unseen. His spelling reminded me of something and I wondered if he'd gone to the same school as his dad.

Carefully pulling the pins out, I pushed the note into my coat pocket and went inside.

I knew before I closed the door that something wasn't right. The remaining books and records had been flung across the passageway like someone big and heavy had smashed into the bookcase. The rug in the hall was rucked up and the coat rack lay in two pieces. But it was the size twelve Dr Marten boot protruding from the open living room door that made my guts perform a quick tango while my shoes did a moonwalk back onto the landing. It wasn't necessary to see the rest of him to know who was occupying my floor space and I didn't need to be a fortune teller to predict he wasn't going to be waking up anytime soon.

I stood for a moment trying to recall if there'd been anything different downstairs: I'd come in through the front and there'd been no sign of forced entry. Mrs Nicholson's plant pots still sat on alternate steps all the way up to the first floor, so apart from Ronnie, whoever else had come up that way had taken care not to disturb anything on the way down.

Of course, that's assuming the intruder had actually left.

I peered back into the passage. The foot was still there, sticking up like it had been nailed in place to stop it falling over. Reaching round, I picked up one of the few items Sharon had left behind and advanced towards the living room. Holding it like an axe, ready to wallop the killer (who was surely standing behind a door waiting in murderous anticipation), I glanced into the bathroom. As Sharon had taken the shower curtain there was no possibility of a Psycho moment. I looked into the bedroom, but the mirror on the opposite wall told me it too was empty. Keeping to the left hand wall and wishing I'd done the sensible thing and called the police, I took another three steps and peered into the kitchen. Like the previous rooms, it was free of murderers, though if I'm honest, I'd already worked out that anyone with a grain of common sense would have realised the only place to hide was behind the living room door.

I took a breath and stepped into the same square of carpet occupied by the boot. Sure enough, the man it belonged to was lying flat out on my floor, his face bashed in with some heavy object. The only good news seemed to be that as the door was pushed back against the wall, whoever had done for him had long since gone.

As I lowered the hockey stick, I realised that not only had I discovered the murder weapon, I'd also just put my fingerprints all over it. A sliver of Big Ronnie's blood slid down the shaft and onto my hand.

Great.

Chapter 2

Charis Brown had been the best-looking girl at my school. She was small and graceful, with an elfin-like smile and eyes that could melt a Mr Whippy at fifty paces. She was the sort of girl who'd have a sly fag behind the bike sheds, then blame someone else when she got caught. She wasn't the sort of girl to go to Hendon and work her way up to Detective Inspector. Or rather, she was. Apparently.

When the shock of seeing her had worn off a little, I stepped back and let her into the flat. The two plods in the living room were still taking notes and the scene of crime bloke was still doing whatever scene of crime blokes do. I backed into the kitchen and offered coffee.

'Didn't know you lived round here,' said Inspector Brown.

'Didn't know you were interested.' I was aiming for gentle humour but only managed cynicism.

She glanced into the room opposite. 'Friend of yours?'

'Not exactly.'

She crossed to the living room and had a few words with the taller of the plods. They glanced back at me a few times, but as coppers always make me nervous, I couldn't tell if that was a good thing or not.

Charis came back and leaned on the counter.

'You used to work for him, didn't you?' It wasn't really a question.

I nodded. 'For him and his dad, yes.' I poured the coffee and slid the milk carton along the counter. 'Only gave it up a few weeks back.'

'Funny.' She helped herself to a Custard Cream.

'What is?'

'That two stiffs turn up in less than twenty-four hours and you're connected to both of them.'

A bad feeling started to make a name for itself in my stomach. The sort of bad feeling I'd been expecting, but was hoping might've buggered off before the police arrived. 'You talking about Frank?'

'Aye.' Her face had lost its elfin-like charm.

'Hardly the same thing - he didn't get his face bashed in, for a start...'

'Maybe not, but he's still dead.' Her dark eyebrows knitted together and she peered into her mug as if searching for a clue. 'Bit of a coincidence don't you think?'

'What ye sayin, like?' I hoped I sounded more comically-offended than I felt.

She gave me a long, hard look. 'I'm like that Sherlock Holmes - I'm not fond of coincidences. In fact, I'd be willin to bet they don't exist.' She took her coffee through to the other room and stood in the doorway watching the guy in the paper suit, who appeared to be dipping cotton buds into Ronnie's face.

I wanted to ask how she knew about Frank - after all, heart attacks are hardly police business. I had the feeling I wasn't getting the full story and the old-school-pals bit wouldn't be enough to cut a deal.

Sipping my Alta Rica, I looked out of the kitchen window. A few of my neighbours had huddled together in the lane at the end of the gardens, a couple of golf umbrellas keeping them relatively dry. No doubt they'd be venting their spleens on the myriad reasons why half a dozen coppers were trawling through my dustbins, taping off my rear entrance and asking all the usual awkward questions.

Inspector Brown coughed. 'Got somewhere to stay, have ye?'

'Why would I need somewhere to stay?'

She jerked her head to the murder scene. 'They'll be hours yet.'

'That's all right.'

She sighed. 'No, what I'm sayin is, you need to go somewhere else. At least for tonight.' She held out a hand, palm up, wiggling her fingers. I noticed there was no wedding band.

'What?'

'Fuck's sake, Terry, I don't want to play with your bollocks. Give me your keys.'

I coughed and felt myself flush. 'Right.' Detaching the flat keys from the bunch, I handed them over.

'Better let me have your mobile number as well. And the address of where you'll be.'

I rooted around for a piece of paper, scribbled down the information, folded the sheet in half, then half again, aware of the slight tremor in my hand. Passing it over, I ventured, 'Must've been quick with the autopsy?'

She inclined her head to one side.

I coughed again. 'I mean, with Frank.'

'Hasn't been done yet.'

'So how..?'

She glanced across the passage, then took a step towards me. 'Let's just say we've reason to be interested.'

I posed a couple more exploratory questions, but she wasn't budging, so I got permission to pick up a few things from the bedroom and stuffed them in the bag I'd packed earlier.

At the front of the house, a uniformed constable stood by the door. He gave me a nod as I passed and I was glad to see the rain was slowing up - unlike my neighbours, I didn't play golf.

Jessie's house was on the nicer side of town, where the accountants and wankmanagers lived, in the relative splendour of what the Americans like to call a 'gated community'.

Tudor Grange, with its spotless driveways and manicured hedges, wasn't what I'd call a des res, but the extra bedrooms meant houseguests were easier to accommodate than in the compact and bijou restrictions of Otterburn Terrace.

I parked the car around the side of the house, since Jessie didn't like her neighbours' visual experiences to be marred by the economic limitations of a bog-standard Japanese ex-taxi.

'You're late.'

My sister never said hello. Come to think of it, I couldn't remember a time when she'd said goodbye. This greeting, however, was a new one.

'Late for what?' I walked past her into the wide entrance hall.

'You were coming for lunch. Remember?' She stood, hands on hips, her mouth set in the almost permanent sneer that passed for smiling.

'Ah, sorry. Forgot.'

'I expect you've got a good excuse.' And she moved off into the kitchen, the space she always favoured in my company. I liked to think it was something to do with growing up in a small and claustrophobic mid-terrace in the Seventies, but it was more likely she just didn't want me contaminating her perfect lounge.

I dished up the potted version of recent events and to her credit, she managed to look suitably aghast.

'Christ, Terry man, what've ye got yerself into?'

I noticed she'd slipped out of her 'posh Geordie' voice and into the working class version she so deplored in others, but on this occasion I didn't bother pointing it out.

'I haven't got meself into anythin, Jess, it's just a misunderstandin.' I watched her spoon Italian beans into the grinder and pondered on the wisdom of pouring another jug of caffeine down my throat, but it was either that or alcohol and I wanted to keep a clear head.

She gave me the usual lecture on mixing with 'that load of tossers' at Ron's Taxis, then wanted to know why I hadn't found another job yet. It was a fair point - forty grand wouldn't last long and as I wasn't known for my ability to talk myself into work, eventually I'd need to get back to the treadmill. Though not for a few weeks.

I changed the subject. 'Where's his lordship?'

She sniffed and pressed the button on the grinder, making conversation impossible. Watching the beans banging around in the hopper, I realised Jessie had a gadget for everything. I wouldn't be surprised if she found a replacement for David one of these days.

'He's at church.'

'Gone to repent his sins?' It was meant as a joke, but she didn't smile.

'He's supervisin work at St. Johns. They're puttin a new roof on and ripping the insides out.'

I wasn't a fan of David any more than he was a fan of mine, but he always made the effort to pretend he liked me - a talent I envied a little too much. We spent an hour or so watching a bit of unreality TV, then when David came home, Jess produced a spontaneous three-course meal.

We moved through to the dining room and I wondered if they always ate in there, sitting in silence, staring at each other from opposite ends of the table. The conversation was sporadic and I felt obliged to entertain, but the effort of relating my tale yet again got the better of me and I gave in to the lure of alcohol. To his credit, David did his best to make enthusiastic replies and relevant comments. After Jessie sloped off to bed, the two of us sat for a while in the living room listening to Mozart.

I was onto my second bottle of Pinot Grigio, so probably wasn't being terribly attentive. However, I did listen to David's woeful tales of building contracts and the difficulties of keeping things going through the winter months. Apart from the shit-load of money he made, it sounded like a difficult life and I was pleased I'd never taken up his offers of labouring work.

'You see, Terry, what ordinary mortals like yourself don't understand, is that the building game isn't about bricks and mortar any more.'

'It isn't?'

'No, it's about politics. Pure and simple. You should come down to the site some time - I'll show ye round.' He was pissed now and I felt my brain closing down as he chuntered on about his latest contract on the Farmway estate on the other side of town. I might have been interested if he'd refrained from quoting hourly rates and tax initiatives at me, but when he changed the subject and started on about how Jess wasn't doing her bit in the bedroom and he was having to look elsewhere for a decent shag, I thought it was time to go.

I drained the last of the Pinot and went to bed.

The next morning it took me a few seconds to

remember where I was and several more to recall my reasons for being there. I checked my mobile: I'd missed three calls from an unknown number, though the necessity of relieving myself of a full bladder took precedence over listening to my voicemails.

It was a long walk to the toilet at the other end of the landing, but the room gave me a view of the front garden and, as it turned out, a hint of what was to come. I assumed the position and unfilled myself while peering through the unfrosted half of the bathroom window. I could see Jessie sweeping leaves into a pile. She was talking to someone across the driveway. As my sister turned and headed back to the house, the newcomer came into view. It was Inspector Brown and she had a child with her. That'd be the missed calls, then.

I'd forgotten to bring a complete set of toiletries, so using one of Jessie's supply of spare toothbrushes, I brushed my teeth twice in a bid to vanquish the taste of excess alcohol from my breath. I looked at myself in the faux art deco mirror that sat on the wall above an art nouveau washbasin. The clash of artistic styles was testament to Jessie's abundance of money and unfortunate lack of taste. Nevertheless, the mirror worked fine and my face looked better than it felt, which was about as good as I was going to get. Back in the bedroom, I grabbed a few items from my bag, pushed it back under the bed and got dressed.

'The police are here.' Jessie was half way up the

stairs and glaring at me like I'd dropped a clanger. Which I suppose I had, if you assumed a visit from the fuzz counted as bringing disrepute upon the neighbourhood. Oh, well.

The visitors had been ushered into the conservatory, presumably so the neighbours would think we were simply entertaining guests. I migrated towards the armchair in the corner - the only comfortable seat in the room.

Charis introduced me to her child: 'This is Detective Constable Paul Ramshaw.' The youngster nodded at me without making eye contact. His boss continued. 'We've a few more questions to ask you Mr Bell.' She gestured to the obligatory rattan sofa. 'Okay if we sit down?' I wondered if the formal approach was for my benefit or Constable Child's.

Jess hovered in the doorway miming, Shall I make coffee? I gave her a Yes please! sign and she scurried off.

'Right then,' said the inspector. 'How about you tell us exactly what you were doing the evening before last?' She took out a small black notebook. Her sidekick copied her actions. I wondered if they'd compare notes later.

'Friday, you mean?'

'That would be the evening before last, yes.'

Going to be like that, then. I sniffed and made on I was thinking about it.

Charis raised an eyebrow, her pen at the ready.

'Well, normally I'd have been on the rank from about 4.00pm, but —'

'But you weren't?'
'No. I weren't.' She didn't smile. 'I was working on the car.'
'All night?'
I nodded. 'Til about nine o'clock, half-nine. Car needed a service, ye know, so...brakes, filters. That sort of thing.' I glanced at the child, then for good measure added, 'I had to take the meter and radio out as well, and remove the plates.'

The teenage constable leant forwards. 'That's the taxi meter and the two-way radio you rented from Ron's Taxis in your service as a Hackney carriage driver?' He inclined his head and for a moment I thought he was going to smile winsomely.

'That's right.'

Inspector Brown glanced at her colleague and I sensed some pre-planned strategy. She looked at me. 'That's strange, because the hackney plates are quite clearly still on your car. So you didn't take them back to the taxi company, did you? In fact, as you'd resigned your position as a driver with the firm three weeks ago, you should have returned all the equipment then.'

I swallowed hard. 'I should have, yes.'

'But you didn't.'

This was getting a little repetitive. 'No, I didn't. What's your point?'

'My point, Mr Bell, is that maybe you wanted a reason to visit Ronnie's Taxis yesterday morning?'

'I already had a reason - to tell Ken about Frank.' I glanced at the sidekick. He was scribbling away furiously on his pad, as if he couldn't fill the pages quick enough. 'Am I missing somethin here?'

'Why did you go to see Ronnie Thompson?'

'You know why - I've just told you. Anyway, Ronnie wasn't there.'

'So you knew Ronnie wasn't around?'

'How could I know Ronnie wasn't around? As you pointed out, I don't work for him anymore.'

She leaned back and let out a long sigh. 'You and Ronnie didn't get on.'

'Not so's you'd notice.'

'But you still went out of your way, knowing he might be there yesterday morning?'

There was a polite cough from the doorway and Jessie was hovering again, this time carrying a tray.

'That's very kind of you,' said the constable, taking it from her. He stood for a moment unsure what to do with it. Eventually he opted for lowering it to the ground then made a dick of himself trying to fill three cups from his crouched position.

Jess caught my eye and half-smiled in a rare example of familial concern. She left the door open and disappeared back into the kitchen.

Charis took her cup and leaned forward, balancing it between her knees. 'In the statement you gave to Constable Riley yesterday you said you'd gone to the taxi office on Saturday morning at the behest of Mrs Armstrong.'

I nodded and sipped my coffee. 'That's right. To tell them about Frank.'

'You said Mrs Armstrong called you.'

I nodded.

'And what time was that?'

Not having a naturally suspicious mind, I didn't see where this was going. 'I dunno. About seven-thirty, maybe.'

Charis glanced at her colleague again, and I saw that same look pass between them.

'So you went round to Rothesay Terrace and Mrs Armstrong let you in?'

'Yes. Well, no, not exactly. The door was open.'

The constable shuffled forward, sweat glistening on his brow. 'So you found the body?' The gleam in his eye told me what I'd been missing.

'No, Lizzy was there. She found him and called me.'

'Why would she call you, Mr Bell?'

'Have you asked her?'

'I have, and now I'm asking you.'

I took a breath and felt it catch in my throat as I struggled for an explanation. 'Well, she just...I mean, she wanted, you know, someone there...'

The youngster persisted. 'Someone there?'

'Yes. I mean, for God's sake, if someone close to you had just died, you wouldn't want to be on your own, would you?'

He leaned back as if his job was done.

'So you're saying Mrs Armstrong was already in the house when you arrived?' Charis's mouth went into a kink at one side, in a sort of pretend smile.

I dropped my head, like I was getting bored. 'Yes.'

The chair creaked as she sat back and I could feel her eyes burning into me. Then, 'Did you notice anything unusual when you entered the house?'

'You mean apart from the fact that Frank was lying dead on his dining room table?' I tried to remember my first impression of the room when I'd seen him laid out, but all I could think was that it looked exactly like it had every other time I'd been in the house, except for the body.

And then I remembered something, but as Charis hadn't mentioned it, I thought I'd keep it for later. Looking up, I saw from her expression that, as usual, I'd given too much away.

She craned her neck. 'Anything else?'

I shook my head and looked out the window, hoping she'd think I was searching the caverns of my mind for some elusive detail. 'No, nothing I can think of.'

'Right.' And she was on her feet, heading for the door. 'I'll most likely want to see you again,' she said over her shoulder.

The constable followed her, then stopped at the front door, turned and delved into his coat pocket. 'Here.' Throwing the keys across the hall, he waved a finger at me. 'Don't leave town.'

Jess appeared and stood in the doorway, no doubt making sure they were definitely leaving. I headed for the kitchen and opened the fridge.

'What was all that about?' Jess had her arms folded, which was never a good sign.

I grabbed a pack of bacon. 'Fucked if I know. Can

I make a buttie?'

She made a huffing noise. 'How can ye not know - you're the one that's been sitting there talkin to them?' She snatched the bacon off me and switched on the George Foreman grill.

I shook my head. 'There's obviously summat they're not saying.'

'Like what?'

I stared at her. 'I don't know like what, cos they're not saying, are they?'

'Well, ye've got your keys back so you can bugger off home when ye've eaten this.'

'Thanks.'

Back at Otterburn Terrace, I was happy to see the police presence had disappeared, though another, unexpected individual had replaced him. Ken Thompson was sitting on my communal doorstep, elbows on knees, head in hands. He looked about as pleased to see me as Jessie had.

'Ken.'

He rubbed the back of one hand across his face. 'Terry.' As he squinted up at me, the hard line of his mouth told me he wasn't looking to catch up on old times.

I waited while he got to his feet, then opened the front door and waved him inside. Watching his size tens clomping up the stairs to my flat, I couldn't help wonder if this was the first time he'd paid a visit.

Unsurprisingly, the cops hadn't bothered to clear

up, so the broken coat stand still lay on the hall carpet. I threw my coat onto the bed and watched Ken stop at the end of the passage. He stood gazing down at the dark stain on the carpet that marked the spot where his son's head had been caved in.

'Through here, mate.' I took his arm and led him into the kitchen. He leaned against one of the units as if he needed the support.

'The cops don't think ye killed him.' His eyes avoided mine and he looked like he might cry.

'No, I didn't.' It was a little early in the day for alcohol, but I couldn't face making yet more coffee while struggling to conjure up small talk, so I reached into the fridge and handed him a beer.

Ken knocked back half the contents then balanced the can on his ample belly, leaving a wet patch on his shirt. He was wearing the same clothes as the day before and I wondered if he'd been to bed. Raising his eyes to my shoulder, he said, 'I dunno where else to go.'

Though I'd picked him up from his house several times over the previous year, I couldn't quite recall where he lived. I did a mental journey up from the office, through town and over the bridge, then left into one of the Council estates. Second or third on the right and there it was - Sebastopol Street. Nice house, shitty area. There was something else too, something I should have remembered.

'Can't go home,' he muttered. 'It was bad enough living in that house without Beryl, but now...'

Oh yes - the dead wife.

I struggled for supportive phrases, positive, reassuring, but all I could manage was, 'You can always stay here if you like?'

He looked right at me and I waited for the onslaught, the tirade of abuse at the mere thought that his emotions could stand to spend a night in the place where his son was murdered. I felt moderately relieved when he shook his head.

I waited, but he continued to stare at the floor, so ditching the positive and reassuring crap, I went for inoffensive. 'Expect Carol's got things in hand down the road, has she?'

He nodded. 'Aye.'

'Good thing she's there, eh? What with...one thing and another.'

He looked at me. 'Ronnie hated her, you know?'

'Did he?'

He didn't reply and gazed off into the distance. We stood there for ages, avoiding eye contact. The silence was agony and I wondered how long I could stand it without screaming out for conversation. Any normal person would've shut the fuck up, given him space to talk, the chance to get it off his chest etc. If he'd wanted to. And if he didn't, that same regular individual would've just 'been there' for him. But not me. After a couple of minutes, it was too much and I heard myself stammer, 'If there's...you know...anything I can do?'

And there it was - a simple meaningless phrase, a platitude, intended to do nothing more than imply, 'It's all right, mate, I'm here for you.' Not - definitely not - a phrase to be taken literally.

Ken's face brightened, or at least, took on the appearance of a slightly less recently-bereaved taxi driver. 'Well, now you mention it, we are two drivers down.'

Chapter 3

The next morning, I had a pleasurable few minutes staring up at the sun-dappled ceiling, believing I didn't have a damn thing to do. Then I remembered the conversation with Ken.

It was only just after seven, so there was no need to rush. I reckoned I could take my time, have a leisurely breakfast, check emails and whatnot before trotting round to the office to do what I'd agreed to the night before - covering the lunch-to-teatime rush. As I still hadn't actually disconnected the radio from my car, and in fact hadn't removed any of the other items that marked it as a hackney carriage, all I had to do was dig out my cash bag and sort out loose change.

On my way to the lock-up at the end of the street, a blue Rover passed me. I might've been mistaken, but the redhead in the driver's seat looked a lot like Charis. Was she spying on me? Checking up? Or simply proving the non-existence of one of those coincidences she didn't actually believe in?

I slid the magnetic 'Taxi' sign onto the roof above the driver's-side door and plugged it back in. Still worked. My cash bag had plenty loose change and even a couple of fivers I'd forgotten about. Lastly, I made sure my just-in-case spanner was in its usual place under the seat. And that was it - I was a cabbie again.

Shortly after eleven, I drove down the Esplanade and parked up round the corner from the office. Three more Nissan Crappys were in front of me, which meant any cushy jobs would've already gone. Not that I cared - all I wanted was an easy afternoon.

'Thought ye weren't comin back?' Carol flashed me a smile and pushed a clipboard across the counter.

'Don't get any ideas pet, I'm just helpin out.' I filled in my shift details and passed it back. 'Just park up on the rank, then, will I?'

'Can't expect to get the best jobs if you're not here, can ye? Joe was in at eight so he's out on an airport run and Geoff's first on the list for Newcastle.' She nodded towards the office. 'Him and Fat Barry are in with Ken. All a bit bloody secretive for my liking. Don't suppose you know anything about it?'

I glanced at the office door where Geoff and Fat Barry-shaped forms moved around against the frosted glass. Their voices were too low to make out what they were saying, but I could guess the topic of conversation. 'They'll be after Ronnie's share of the account work if I know those two.' I sniffed. 'Where's everyone else? Craig, Beardy Bob an them?'

'Ken's put them on evenings for now. Bob's not happy - nearly had a blue fit when he realised he'd miss out on Monday night bingo.'

'Would've thought he'd be glad to get away from

his missus.' I leaned over the desk. 'You spoken to the police?'

She nodded. 'Aye. Sod's have taken all the job sheets for Friday and Saturday. I canna do me bloody figures til I get them back.'

'Were you on the desk Friday night?'

'I was. Busy enough and there was a fight at The Ferryboat. Geoff ended up taking three blokes to the RVI.'

'What about Frank?'

'What about him?'

'He was working, wasn't he?'

'Well...' She glanced towards the office. 'Ye know Frank, he's normally dead busy, rushing around all over the place, one after another, but that night he only did about ten jobs.' She paused. 'Come to think of it, a couple of them were on the new contract.'

'Sangster?'

She shook her head. 'New one. Ronnie took it on just after you left. Big deal apparently. Him and Ken were dead chuffed, reckoned it was goin to be worth a bomb.'

'Oh aye? What sort of contract?'

'Mostly picking up construction workers from home and dropping them at sites and offices between here and Killingworth, though there's been a few for the company bosses as well - ye know, restaurants and stuff?'

The radio crackled and Carol picked up the mic. 'You clear, Jimmy? That wifie from 49 Inkerman thinks she left something in your car. Can ye pop round there?' She hung up the mic and looked at me. 'That's all I know.'

'Big company, is it?'

'I dunno. They're called SAHB.'

'Sensational Alex Harvey Band?'

She laughed. 'I doubt it. And before ye ask, they're not a car maker either. The boss feller's called Andersson, so it's probably...' She shook her head. 'Something Andersson Something Something.'

'Catchy name. An he's signing the cheques, is he, this Andersson?'

She made a face. 'Come on, Terry, that's confidential. I canna be givin out that sort of information.'

'And what if it's linked to Frank's death?' Admittedly, I had no reason to think this was likely, but it couldn't hurt to check.

Carol hesitated and glanced again at the office door. Dropping her voice to a whisper, she said, 'Look, there's only been one invoice in so far and it had Sven Andersson's signature on it. And hey - I better not get dropped in the shite for tellin ye.'

'So he's a builder?'

She nodded. 'From what they were sayin, it sounds like he's got things going on all over the place. Got his fingers in that new development up past Tesco's an all sorts.'

'I see.' I'd seen construction work taking shape on the patch of land behind the supermarket, but I'd no idea what they were building. From the size of the thing, it might be anything from an apartment block to a new high school. 'Okay, I'll be on the rank if you need me.'

I was almost out onto the landing when she said, 'I hear Sharon's moved out.'

Feeling a sigh coming on, I coughed instead. 'Friday night. Well, yesterday morning, really. Why, like?'

A slow smile spread across her face. 'No reason.'

Outside, a cool breeze was coming in and a hint of the haar that often engulfed the coast at this time of year was making itself felt. The summer was long gone and with any luck, a nice autumn chill would be enough to prompt a few shoppers to take a cab home instead of waiting for a bus.

It was like being on automatic pilot as I drove up to the High Street and pulled onto the back of the taxi rank. There were seven cars in front of me and at this time of day, I knew it might be five minutes or half an hour before I got a fare. Rolling down my window, I stuffed my cash bag into the driver's side pocket, then fished around in the glove compartment to find the novel I'd been reading intermittently for the last month or so. Reading was one of several things I'd planned to do a lot more of when I had the time, along with setting up a Facebook account, updating my email passwords and getting to grips with online banking, but typically, I hadn't got round to it yet.

Ten minutes later, I'd moved to the front of the queue and was well into the misdemeanours of a bent New York cop, when the nearside rear passenger door opened and a little round woman squeezed herself onto the seat, propping a pair of carrier bags on her lap. 'I thought that was you, Terry - where've you been?'

I leaned over the back of the seat. 'Just had a couple of weeks off, Evie. Goin home, are ye?'

She nodded. 'Aye, and divvent spare the horses.'

That first fare was a short run, but as I helped the old woman out with her bags, it felt like I'd never been away.

'Thanks pet,' she said, giving me a cheeky grin. 'Ye can pick me up anytime.'

I watched her into the house then got back in the car just as a blue Rover pulled alongside. The child in the driver's seat wound his window down and signalled for me to do the same.

'Morning Constable Ramshaw,' I said.

'It's Detective Constable. And it's afternoon.'

Condescending prick. 'Thanks for the update. Can I help ye at all?'

'Back on the cabs, then?'

'Temporarily.' I leaned forward and made a show of noticing he was alone. 'Charis let you out by yourself, has she?'

His reply was lost as the car pulled away. I watched him disappear round the corner and wondered if he'd just happened to be passing, or if he'd been checking up on me. Again.

The rest of the afternoon was relatively busy and by the time I'd called in my last pickup I'd had enough and was ready for home. I clicked the radio again. 'Car ten signing off.'

'Can ye pop up to the office for five minutes Terry?' Carol's voice sounded odd, but maybe she was just stressed - couldn't be easy running things just now.

It was after six when I bumped the car up onto the pavement in front of the office. Maybe Ken had decided he didn't want me here after all. Maybe he'd left Carol to pass on the good news. I made plenty of noise going up the stairs, just in case they were all up there talking about me. But they weren't. A young couple busied themselves eating each other's faces while they waited for a driver. Carol was at the desk wearing a tight smile.

'Okay?'

She nodded, but she wasn't her usual cheery self and there was something else in her expression I couldn't quite read.

'Can ye do one last job before you go?'

I nodded. 'Sure. These two?' I indicated the snoggers.

'No.' She passed a note across the desk. 'Just a pickup from the Hexagon. Dropping off at Central Station.'

I looked at the note. 'Thought ye said –'

'You'll need to get a signature.'

Shaking my head, I put the note back on the desk. 'I told Ken I wouldn't be doing any account work.'

'Aye, but it's that new contract and...and they asked for you. Specially.'

'Really?'

'Maybe an old customer?'

'Old customer on a new account? Doesn't seem likely.' I stared at her but she'd swivelled back to the radio, fiddling with the log sheets. I picked up the job slip again and looked at the name - Elise. 'No surname?'

She shrugged. 'Didn't say. Might be one of the bosses at SAHB.'

I waited til she turned around. 'Did Ken authorise this?'

She pouted. 'Look, Terry, they asked for you. I'm just doin what I'm told.'

'Think this might be who Frank picked up on Friday?'

'If I had the job sheets I could tell ye, but I haven't, all right?' She was beginning to sound irritated.

'So he could have?'

'I've told yer - I don't know. When the cops bring me stuff back I can have a look.'

Studying the name again, I knew I wasn't going to be able to resist finding out who this woman was - and more to the point, why she'd asked for me. If it turned out she knew something...

'Fine, I'm going.' I stopped at the door. 'If I wake up dead tomorrow, I'll be really annoyed.'

Carol smiled despite herself. 'I wouldn't worry - it's probably yet another one of your many ex-girlfriends.'

'Aye,' I said, solemnly. 'I expect it is.'

The Hexagon was one of those fancy modern designs that never looks right in a northeast town. True to its name, the six-sided structure balanced precariously on the edge of the cliff like an alien craft that hadn't quite landed. It reminded me of the house that American architect knocked up - the one that sticks out over the waterfall.

The style of the thing did nothing to compliment the surrounding architecture, though maybe that was the point. The recent passion for regenerating all things pre-Sixties, had taken off in a big way after the area fell into disrepute along with the rest of the town. Though the nearby shops and offices had at least regained something of their former glory, this place looked more like something that should've been built on Canary Wharf. The rising fog added an air of eerie mystery that I might have thought was interesting if I was a fan of film-noir.

I parked outside the front door and immediately a gorilla wearing shades strode over and leaned into the car.

'No pickups here, mate.' He pointed along the street. 'Go into the car park and see the attendant.'

I sighed and did as I was told.

The attendant turned out to be an old guy in a red apron with a matching cap and a badge declaring Here to Help! The American influence was clear. He crouched down and gave me a tired smile.

'All right marra? Who yer lookin for?'
'Elise.'

'Elise Andersson?'

'Could be.'

He raised an eyebrow. 'Picked her up before?'

'No, first time.'

He leaned inside the car so his nose was almost touching mine. 'Word of warnin - she's a fancy bit of stuff, but divvent try anythin, or ye'll end up sitting on the Dogger Bank wi' your heid in your hands.'

'Thanks for the advice.' I watched him cross to the steps and speak to a young man who went off in search of my client. While I was waiting, I pulled out my phone and Googled the man whose contract I was fulfilling. Turned out it was a common name - certainly too many to look through without a couple of hours to spare. I tried the name of the company and came up trumps for rock bands, but the only website that looked likely to be my guy was 'under construction'. Aye, right.

A door slammed and I looked up to see the vision of loveliness that was Elise Andersson standing in the doorway. The apron wearer led her over to my car and opened the door.

'Good evening,' I said, being polite.

She stared at me in a way that seemed to suggest I should shut the fuck up and drive. So I did.

It was a half-hour run to the town at that time of night and the coast road was in that cooling-off period between folks racing home from work and on their way out to the pub. I kept an eye on my passenger but she seemed happy enough to stare out the window. She was certainly good looking and the dress she wasn't quite wearing wouldn't have looked out of place on the cat-walk. I guessed her age to be about thirty-five but without a closer look, I wasn't going to stake my life on it.

As we hit the early evening traffic it occurred to me she didn't have a coat or any baggage - apart from one of those ineffectual clutch bags. I was tempted to point out she'd catch her death if she walked around half naked, but the attendant's warning kept my inquisitiveness at half mast.

Twenty-five minutes later, I slid into line at the train station and was about to jump out and open her door when the Swedish goddess sat forward and tapped my shoulder.

'Can you take me somewhere else?'

Her voice was like silk sheets on a glass bed - smooth and cold. I turned to look at her. 'The job was just to bring you here. To the station.'

'Yes, but I want to go somewhere else.' She reached into her bag and pulled out a scrap of paper. 'Can you take me here?'

I peered at the address. It was a street in Elswick. Not an area I'd recommend to classy people like her. Not an area I'd recommend to anyone. 'All right then, but I can't wait around.'

She shrugged. 'It's fine - my husband will pick me up.'

I manoeuvred the car out of the line and back into the westbound lane. 'What about the fare? It's going to be more.'

'I'll pay the extra in cash. Don't put it on the

receipt.'

'Okay.' It was getting dark now and I couldn't see her face clearly, but her demeanour had definitely changed. And since now I was doing her a favour, I reckoned she might be open to answering one or two questions.

Five minutes later, I turned into a side road and slowed down so I could see the doors. 'What number is it?'

'Here will do fine.'

She waited while I wrote out a receipt. After embellishing it with her signature, she handed it back together with a twenty-pound note. 'That will cover it?'

'More than enough.' I stuffed it into my cash bag before she changed her mind. She already had the door open so I jumped in quick. 'Why did you ask for me?'

She hesitated and blinked several times. 'I didn't.'

'Whoever booked the taxi mentioned my name.'

She gave a slight shrug.

I tried another tack. 'I think one of my mates might have picked you up the other night.'

She slid one leg out the door and looked back. 'Mates?'

'Yeah, Frank. Older guy, grey hair.'

She pursed her lips and gave the smallest of nods.

'Bring you here, did he?'

'I think that's enough questions.' She climbed out of the car and disappeared through a gate. A moment later, a light came on and I caught a glimpse of a tall bald-headed man before the door closed.

I drove a little way down the street, reversed round the next corner and stopped. Basically, I was none the wiser. All I'd found out was that she'd met Frank and he may or may not have picked her up on Friday night and he may or may not have brought her here.

I drove back up the road and out onto the main drag. Two hundred yards along, I parked up outside a pub, walked back to Nugent Crescent and nipped down a narrow path at the side of the first house. As I'd suspected, it was one of those streets with an alley behind it that backed onto the yards of the next row. Since I didn't know what number I'd dropped her at, I had to guess at the location of the house. The darkness and lack of streetlights meant I probably wouldn't be observed, but it also meant I couldn't see where the hell I was going. About half way along the lane, I noticed one house in particular was lit up more than the others. As if there might be something special going on.

Most of the properties had high wooden gates on them, so it wasn't easy to see into the ground-level rooms. However, the lit-up house had a well-placed baton across the lower section of its gate and I was able to clamber up high enough to see over the top. Keeping low, I peered over the edge. There was a long yard area at the back of the house with a couple of motorbikes chained to the wall. Between them and the house itself was a sort of patio with one of those swinging chairs, a table and chairs and a brick-built barbecue. The house was double width with the back door in the middle and two floor-to-ceiling windows that left nothing to the imagination. A dozen or so people milled around in both the downstairs rooms, though it was the performance going on upstairs that caught my attention.

Wafts of dark fabric were draped over the windows, but thanks to the well-lit rooms, they weren't hiding much. At the left-hand window, a woman looking remarkably like Ms Andersson had her back to the glass. Either side of her were two Asian guys with big smiles. Both of them had their shirts open as if in the throes of undressing.

My voyeuristic activities were rudely interrupted when something hard and boot-like slammed into my right leg. I did a vaguely athletic move along the lines of a Fosbury Flop, before landing on the ground with a thud.

Chapter 4

'What da fuck you doin, man?'

I looked up at my attacker and scooted backwards, in case he intended having another go, but he just laughed.

'It's cool, man. Just messin witcha.'

I reckoned he wasn't actually African American, given he was wearing a flat cap and a pair of Dunlop wellies.

'What the hell was that for?' I scrambled to my feet and glanced around, but we were alone.

'Dat Mister Ahmed'll smack you up good if catches ye, man. Good fing me found yer first, hey?' His accent shifted from generic black American into a weird version of Jamaican Cockney.

'Ahmed, you say? He the baldy bloke?'

'Nah, that's Crazy Horse.' He paused. 'You wantin ter know why they call him Crazy Horse, yeh? I'll tell yer for why - cos he's crazy and has a cock like a horse.' He laughed again, though now it seemed like he was trying too hard.

'You must be on intimate terms.'

His face fell and he sneered. 'Wit him? Nah. Bastard caught me trying to nick one of them bikes one night. Thought he'd just smack me up or sumfink, but nah. Know what he did? Bent me over a wheelie bin and tried to stuff his dick up me arse. An he would've done an'all if I hadn't elbowed him in the guts.'

I blinked. 'I see.'

He shook his head. 'Nah, man, I don't fink you do. I got off dead light that time. One of me mates, yeh, he broke inter the guy's garage one time and I ain't never seen him again. What I'm sayin is if'n you mess wit those fuckers you'll get well fucked, yeh?' He nodded sagely.

'Who lives there? Just Mister Ahmed?'

He took my arm and led me along the lane. 'Don't want ter 'ang about 'ere, or they'll see yer.' We walked a little further then he pulled me to one side. 'That Ahmed - he hardly never goes nowhere, but there's loads of women an that in an out all night. Fellers too, mind. It's like they's always having parties an that, yeh?'

'What sort of parties?'

'I dunno. Never got close enough to find out.' He peered at me. 'What's your interest, man? What you doin here?'

'Just dropped someone off, that's all. Then I got curious.'

He shook his head. 'If I was you, I'd leave curious alone, mate, less'n you want bits of you to go missin an that, yeh?'

He glanced back along the lane. 'Look, I'm off. You go that way and don't walk round the front.' He patted my shoulder then skipped across the lane and scrambled over the fence opposite.

I pondered on going back for another look, but wasn't keen on bumping into the man called Horse, so I followed my new friend's instructions, walked down to the end of the lane and round to the left, then circled up to the main road.

Back in the car, I sat for a moment considering what I'd learned. Or rather, what I hadn't learned. If this Ahmed bloke was dangerous why would Frank have got involved with him? Frank wasn't known for taking risks - putting salt on his fish 'n' chip supper was about as dangerous as he got. The only reason he might have been drawn in, was if a woman was being threatened. That was his soft spot. In fact, if I remembered rightly, that was how he'd met Lizzy. She'd climbed into his cab one night with a particularly aggressive guy in tow. The pair were arguing about something and when the guy started slapping Lizzy around, Frank bopped him over the head with his fire extinguisher.

Nevertheless, I couldn't see Frank walking into a place like Ahmed's without a damn good reason.

I was still sitting there contemplating this when Carol's voice came over the radio.

'Car ten? You clear yet, Terry?'

I called in and told her I was on my way home. She clicked the radio twice in reply, meaning she was on the phone and couldn't respond. I was just about to set off back when a vaguely familiar tinkling noise caught my attention. Since communications from actual people were something of a rarity, it took me a moment to work out that the pinging noise was in fact a text message. It was Carol:

Come round to mine when you get back. Got some news.

I wasn't sure from the text if this 'news' was likely to cheer me up, but as I'd never been in Carol's flat, it was as good a reason as any to have a nosy.

Driving back, I used the time to go over everything that had happened since Friday, but I couldn't see an obvious explanation for Ronnie's murder. If my inspector friend decided to share what she knew, maybe I'd be able to put it together, as whatever additional info they had, they were obviously keeping to themselves.

It was gone half seven when I pulled up outside Carol's place on Crimea Walk. Looking up at the bay window, I guessed that must be her living room. A telltale flicker lit up the window. She was watching telly, though knowing her, it'd be a box-set of some crass American sitcom. I rang the bell and she buzzed me in.

'Took your time.' She left the door open and went into the kitchen to refill her own glass and pour one for me. 'Hope you don't mind, it's only cheap chardonnay.'

I took a sip. 'Tastes fine to me.' I followed her through to the lounge, noting she'd changed out of the jeans and jumper she wore to work and was now wearing a pair of smart leggings and a silk blouse. Maybe that's what she always wore at home, but I preferred the theory that it was for my benefit. The room was tastefully decorated with a cosy lived-in feeling I'd've liked my own place to have.

The floorboards were sanded and a couple of pretend Persian rugs completed the arrangement.

Plonking myself down at one end of a lumpy sofa, I half-expected her to sit next to me. But she didn't. Instead, she walked back and forward a few times, sipping her wine.

It was pretty obvious there was something on her mind.

Eventually, she crossed to the built-in wall unit that doubled as a kind of Welsh dresser and bookcase, and took a piece of paper from between two books.

'When I got home, this was pinned to my door.'

I took the folded sheet and opened it out. I read it twice then stood up and searched through my coat pockets for the note I'd found pinned to my own door. Spreading the two sheets on Carol's dining table, I stood back.

'You got one as well?'

'Saturday. I'd assumed it was from Ronnie.'

Carol leaned on the table and studied the notes. I stood beside her, re-reading them. Mine was short and to the point:

Give it back or youll get whats comin to you

Carol's was even shorter:

Give it back!!

'What's it mean, Terry?' Her hand went to her

mouth. 'What'd you do?'

'Me? I didn't do 'owt.' I turned and leaned against the table. 'Anyway, if this is about me, why did you get one?'

She shook her head.

I took the two notes and went back to the sofa. After a moment, Carol joined me.

Studying the handwriting, which I'd logically thought to be my former employer's, it was obvious. 'It's the same - whoever wrote my note, also wrote this one.'

Carol made a humphing noise. A crease worked its way down her forehead. 'Why did you think it was Ronnie?'

I explained about seeing him approaching my flat, but Carol shook her head. 'If you thought it was him that wrote it, why didn't you give the note to the cops?'

Good point. 'It might have incriminated me.'

Her mouth dropped open. 'How?'

I looked at the note again. 'I thought it referred to me still having the meter and radio in the car. Ronnie texted me a few days ago demanding I give them back.'

'And you didn't?'

'He still owed me for those Sangster jobs I did last month. Which is why I didn't want to do any contract work.' I glared at her.

She pulled a face. 'Fuck's sake. Ken would've given you the money.'

'Yeah, but that's not the point. And I can hardly

ask him now. Given the circumstances.'

We sat for a moment, then Carol turned to face me. 'But still, somebody must think you did something?'

'No, I don't think it's what I did, I think it's what Frank did. Or what somebody thinks he did.'

She picked up my note and looked at it again. 'But this was on your door, so it must've been meant for you.'

I nodded. 'Well, it looks that way, except that now you've got one.'

'Maybe the first note was for Ronnie?' She grabbed my arm. 'What if someone followed him to yours and thought it was his place? And then...'

'Smashed his head in with a hockey stick and pinned a note to the door that he clearly wasn't going to be reading since he was already dead?'

She blinked. 'What hockey stick?'

Fuck.

The sofa wasn't as uncomfortable as it looked, though I couldn't help thinking I'd have been much happier sleeping in Carol's bed. With Carol. But she'd dropped no hints, obvious or otherwise, that anything like that was going to be happening. The only reason she wanted me to stay the night was because some psycho bastard was out there with (probably), a ticky-list of psycho-type inclinations.

On the other hand, it could be she hadn't quite believed my story about the hockey stick, which was fair enough, given that it was the murder weapon. And explaining it to her, I could see how it must've sounded - my prints all over it (despite the fact I'd handled it loads of times before), and Ronnie's blood dripping down the handle onto my sleeve (that was never going to look good), but mainly because whoever had come into my flat and smashed Ronnie's head in, hadn't come armed with a weapon. And anyone intending to commit murder would have thought of that, wouldn't they? Whereas me - I didn't need a weapon, did I? Not when there was already one there.

Well, that was my theory - that the cops would jump to conclusions and I'd end up in the crap. And that's why I'd hidden the hockey stick. Thinking about it now, though, in terms of extenuating circumstances, it sounded a bit flimsy and I wondered if I was making things too complicated.

I lay there in the dark, contemplating the two notes. If they weren't written by Ronnie (and at least one of them couldn't have been), then someone else had been up to the flat, and that same someone had also caved Ronnie's head in and left the note. And then they'd come round to Carol's and left a note for her. Or me. Except, if the first one was meant for Ronnie, it must have been left before he was murdered. But if either or both messages were intended for me, none of that made sense. So did that mean two people were involved? Without knowing who wrote the notes, the missing pieces of this particular jigsaw seemed likely to continue to remain conspicuous by their absence.

As I stared up at the ceiling, I remembered something else.

Knocking on Carol's door, I hoped she wouldn't think I was after a shag, but she was there in an instant and clearly wide awake.

'Can't sleep either?'

I shook my head, gazing down at her polka dot pyjamas. 'You said the Andersson pickup had specifically requested me. Was that true?'

She frowned. 'Course it was - why would I lie?'

'You spoke to the person who called?'

'Ahm...yeah, must have.'

'So who was it and what did they say?'

She studied the floor for a moment. 'It was a bloke. I assumed it was one of the waiters - usually is from that place. He said Elise needed a car on the Andersson account to take her to Central Station and could they have Mister Bell.' She shrugged. 'Maybe you've picked them up before?'

'What, before Ronnie negotiated the contract, you mean?'

'Oh, yeah, I forgot. But still, the contract's for a company so maybe some of their workers know you. Could've picked them up off the rank, maybe?'

I thought about this for a moment. 'Possibly, but I definitely haven't seen Elise before - I'd've remembered her.'

'Oh aye - got big tits, has she?' She gave me an accusatory glare.

'I just mean she's not someone I'd forget. Don't suppose you know what this Sven bloke looks like?'

'Never met him. You could Google him.'
'Already did - there's millions of Anderssons.'
Carol was quiet for a moment then her eyes lit up. 'Hang on - Ken was reading an article about him in the News Post the other day. I'm sure there was a picture of this Sven bloke.'
'Great! Have you got a copy?'
She shook her head. 'Not here, but I know where we can get one.'

Ordinarily, I'd consider it a bit daft to go out in the middle of the night looking for a newspaper, but I needed to know what this bloke looked like, then at least I'd recognise him if we ever bumped into each other. In any case, it was Monday and Mondays were like Tuesdays, and Tuesdays were about as exciting as a wet weekend in Blyth.

It was gone two o'clock when we got to the office. Carol let us in, but left the lights off in case some nosy copper thought the place was being burgled. I closed the door and followed her up the stairs.

With only the orangey glow of the streetlight on the corner to light up the room, the place had an eeriness to it that didn't sit well with me - especially given the events of the past few days. Carol wasn't worried, though, and started rummaging through the files and papers on the counter. Meanwhile, I looked through the magazines and newspapers Ken supplied for the delight of the punters.

The News Post was a weekly broadsheet that had held onto its format through several changes of ownership. It was the place to go for local gossip and political shenanigans, but if you wanted hard facts it was best avoided. There were a few old copies on the coffee table, but Carol reckoned the one we wanted was the issue from the previous week, and naturally, that's the one that was missing.

'I think we've had it.' Carol straightened up and sighed. 'It was worth a shot.'

'Hang on,' I said. There was still another possibility. I tried the door to Ken's office. It opened and I pushed it wide. The place had been trashed and there were files and ledgers all over the floor, but it was the man sitting in the boss's chair with a knife in his chest that drew my attention.

Behind me, Carol let out a low moan. 'Aw, ye're fuckin jokin.'

Chapter 5

Sitting in the back of the police car wasn't a new experience for me, but it freaked the hell out of Carol. She gripped my arm and didn't let go while we sat there watching the cop circus invade the street. Forty minutes after my call, Charis arrived and climbed into the front passenger seat.

'You're beginning to piss me off, Terry,' she said, with only a smidgen of humour. She glanced at Carol and I could see her making assumptions. 'And I suppose,' she went on, 'neither of you have any idea who he is?'

We shook our heads.

'Course not, that would be too easy. Well, at least he isn't dead. Yet.'

Carol was trembling. 'D'you think he'll be all right?'

The inspector shrugged. 'Touch and go, as they say in the movies.' She glanced up at the taxi office. The men in white suits were still inside doing their thing. 'Don't usually get a lot of excitement on a Monday night, though I'd have been just as happy to stay in my bed.'

'What's goin to happen to us?' Carol's voice sounded small and helpless. I put my hand on hers and gave her what I hoped was a reassuring smile.

'I'll need statements from ye's at some point, but ye might as well go home just now.' She hesitated.

'Although, given what's just happened, might be an idea to find somewhere else to stay.' She raised an eyebrow at me and, unfortunately, I knew exactly what she meant.

To say Jessie was not best pleased, wouldn't be over-egging the custard. She stood in the kitchen doorway wearing an extra-large Snoopy t-shirt and a pair of slippers I'd've thought were way too fluffy even for her.

'You do know David's got to be up at six?'

I took a sip of my hot chocolate. 'It wasn't my idea to come here.'

'Maybe not, but you still came.' She sounded angry, even if her face betrayed a softer side. Not much softer, mind, but it gave me a nice warm feeling to know she was probably quite worried about me. Deep down. Nevertheless, she maintained a severe exterior.

'I'm away back to bed. And ye's can make your own fuckin breakfast.' She turned and endeavoured to make a decisive exit, but her slippers caught on the hall carpet and she very nearly fell flat on her face. I didn't laugh until she was out of sight.

'We should've gone to a hotel.' Carol looked up at me, her face less drained than earlier. 'I haven't even got a toothbrush.'

'It's fine. My sister's prepared for any eventuality.'

Upstairs, I showed Carol where she'd be sleeping. There was a toothbrush next to the bed. I pointed to the door along the hall. 'Give us a knock if ye need anything.'

She nodded and closed the door.

Back in what I was now thinking of as 'my' room, I noticed Jessie had changed the sheets as well as the towels. I got ready for bed then switched off the light, but before snuggling down, I crossed to the window. Parting the curtains just enough to peek out, I took in the solitary presence at the end of the driveway. Charis had left one of her plods on guard, but whether he was there to stop us getting out, or to discourage would-be murderers, was anybody's guess.

David and Jessie had already left by the time me and Carol got round to having breakfast. After several cups of coffee, we were ready to face the world, though exactly what it was we'd be facing wasn't clear. Since the police had brought us here, we had no transport. I rang one of our competitors, Coastal Cars. The guy on the desk offered his condolences regarding Frank and Ronnie, though he clearly thought it was hilarious that one of Ronnie's drivers needed a taxi. I told him what had happened the night before and he stopped laughing.

I gathered my things together in the hope we wouldn't have to come back again. Jessie had made it clear we were always welcome, in a not-very-welcoming sort of way. Nevertheless, I still wasn't happy about going back to my flat. Or Carol's, for that matter.

The solitary copper had disappeared by the time we walked down the drive to meet the car. The sleek white Rover made a nice change from Ronnie's unluxurious Nissans, and I wondered if Coastal's made any more money than our drivers. I got the guy to drop us a block away from the office, so that no-one would see us using a rival firm. Thankfully, my car was still parked where I'd left it round the corner, and there were no other cabbies in sight, which indicated those on shift were already on the rank. In any case, they wouldn't have known anything about last night's calamity until they turned up for work. I chucked my gear in the back of the car and we headed for the office.

When we got upstairs, Ken was sitting at the desk with the headphones on, staring into space. His face looked like someone else had slept in it.

'How ye doin?'

His head swivelled towards us and he nodded slowly. 'Been better. You two all right?'

Carol took off her coat and laid it on top of a filing cabinet. 'Never mind us, what about you? You been here all night?' She patted his shoulder.

'Yous must've just left when I arrived. Bloody cops were here til four, buggering about with stuff. Thought I might as well stay.'

I glanced through at the office. 'Did they find out who that bloke was?'

He shook his head. 'Some drunk. They reckon someone must've been up here snoopin about and he came in looking for a cab. One of those wrong place, wrong time whatsits.'

'How did they get in?'

He shrugged. 'Cops reckon they must've picked the lock and left the door open.'

'Did they take anything?'

'Made a fuckin mess, that's for sure. But no, I don't think so.'

It wouldn't have done any good to increase Ken's anxiety level, so I didn't mention that I thought it more likely they hadn't found what they were looking for and would probably come back at some point. Or put another way, it was just another piece of the puzzle that didn't make sense.

He was quiet for a moment, then, 'You okay to work today?'

I nodded. 'So they think he was just unlucky?'

Ken stared at me. 'Unlucky? How the fuck should I know?' He grunted. 'Just one thing after another, isn't it?' He sighed and stood up. 'There you are luv, but if ye need to go home, just say so, all right?'

Carol did her best to smile. 'Course.' She rearranged the magnetic cards on the whiteboard showing who was working and who wasn't, then started going through the booking list.

'Right, looks like Fat Barry and Joe are heading out of town...Jimmy's droppin at Sangster's.' She looked up at me. 'You'd better do this airport run, Terry - it's due in ten minutes.' She scribbled the details on a post-it note and passed it over. 'It was one of Ronnie's bookings, but...'

I glanced at the pickup address. 'Giz a ring if anything happens.'

'What about tonight?'

'I dunno. Maybe you should go an stay with your mam?'

'In friggin Darlington? What about me job?'

I glanced across at Ken, who was watching me closely. 'Think you'd be safer there.' He nodded in agreement.

Carol shook her head. 'Me mam'd drive iz up the wall. I'm better off where I am.'

'Okay. I'll pick you up later. We'll make a decision then.'

The airport pickup was from The Ferryboat Inn, a nice quiet pub on a weekday, though it got a bit rowdy at weekends. Its clientele was more local than touristy and being stuck on the edge of a Council estate, it wasn't the easiest place to find. Being hidden away suited the regulars since most of them favoured a less than honest means of making a living. Also, it wasn't the most obvious place to start from if you had a plane to catch, but I knew the landlord did occasional overnight stays for some of his 'special' customers, so I assumed it was one of those.

The tiny car park was empty and I pulled up at the front entrance. Before I had a chance to open my door, a tall shiny-headed bloke emerged carrying a holdall. He climbed in the back and threw the bag on the seat beside him.

'All right marra?'

'Aye, canny.' I forced myself to drag my eyes away from the rear-view mirror before he noticed I was staring at him. 'To the airport, yeah?'

'That's right bonny lad.' He turned and looked out of the window and I took another quick look at his face. It was him all right - the man who'd welcomed Elise Andersson into the house on Nugent Crescent the night before. Or Mister Crazy Horse, as my recent acquaintance had called him. I pushed the memory out of my mind and tried to come up with a new name for my passenger - one I could associate with a less intimidating image.

I keyed the mic and confirmed I'd picked up. As we pulled away, my passenger tapped me on the shoulder.

'Ronnie not on today?'

I swallowed hard. 'Ahm, no. He's...off sick.'

His eyes narrowed. 'Really? I heard some fucker caved his head in.'

'Oh, aye,' I said, as if I'd just remembered. I cleared my throat, fighting to keep my attention on the road. 'I thought...' Whatever I thought was never going to make it into actual words, so I shut up.

My passenger was staring at me. 'Have we met before?'

'Don't think so.' I took another right and headed towards Sainsbury's and the quickest route out of town.

'So you're not Terry Bell, then?'

The car squealed to a halt and I waved an

apology at the young mother whose kid had almost become minced child. 'Ahm, yes.'

He nodded in a not very reassuring way. 'Aye. That's right - you're the one that dropped Elise off at Ahmed's last night, aren't you?'

I eased the car forward and wondered if there were any friendly policemen in the area. Not that it would've made any difference - if the man in the back of my car was a killer, he was hardly likely to own up to it.

From The Ferryboat, the most direct route took in a few of the back roads that would've made a pleasant drive on any other day. If this guy was planning to bump me off, it also afforded plenty of out-the-way places to do it. Nice quiet woods and fields where a body could be dumped and nobody any the wiser.

'Did ye hear what I said, bonny lad?'

I gulped loudly. 'Oh, aye. Sorry. I was concentrating. Yes, I believe it was me that dropped off...ahm...'

'Elise Andersson.'

'That's right. Elise.' I kept my eyes on the road but I could see his grinning face in my peripheral vision.

'Tell you what...' He leaned forward and rested his humongous arms on the back of my seat. 'Change of plan. I need to pick somethin up at a mate's place.'

'Oh?'

'Aye.' He stretched an arm past my head and I

could smell the polish on his leather coat. A well-manicured finger pointed to a house up ahead. 'See that redbrick place? Turn in there and follow the lane.' He sat back. 'It's not far.' That grinning face again.

I pulled a left where he said, hoping it wouldn't turn out to be a dead end - in every sense of the word. We followed a narrow winding road that led past several houses and a farm. Then Shiny Head leaned forward again.

'Pull in here.'

There was a sort of lay-by ahead, with a gravel track leading up to a grotty-looking house. I brought the car to a halt and waited nervously for further instructions. But my passenger was already heaving his large frame out the door and heading off up the track. For a moment I thought it must be a trick, that he was going to turn around, demand I get out the car then blow me away without further ado. Instead, he strode up to the house and I watched as the door opened and he stepped inside.

The sensible thing to do would be to simply drive away, but if this guy really was involved in Ronnie's death and thought I suspected him, why would he leave me sitting here with an obvious escape route?

So I sat and waited.

Of course, I could be completely wrong. Maybe he'd found himself sans murder weapon and had stopped to pick up a gun/lethal injection/great big fuck-off knife? But if he was a killer, surely he'd have had the great big fuck-off knife in his bag?

Which reminded me - it was still there on the seat where he'd left it. I glanced back up at the house. There was no sign of life and even if he did suddenly appear, it'd take him half a minute or so to get back to the car. Plenty time to root through his luggage and find that magical piece of incriminating evidence to back up my theory.

Keeping half an eye on the house, I reached over and unzipped the holdall. Digging my hand in, I found something soft and clothing-like. Clothes, in fact. I slid my fingers around the sides, but there was nothing remotely hard and gun-like, sharp and pointy or even syringe-shaped - only more clothes.

I fastened the bag back up. Then I noticed it was perched on the edge of the seat. That wasn't where he'd left it. I pushed it back and checked its position in my rear-view mirror. Is that where it had been? I reached over again and pushed it further along. There, maybe? It'd have to do - Head Case was on his way back.

'Still here, then?' he said, getting into the car. 'Thought you might've buggered off.'

'Don't be daft,' I said, trying to laugh, but it sounded unnatural. Looking over my shoulder, I couldn't help catch his eye as I reversed into the driveway and turned the car round. I hoped it was my imagination, but there seemed to be a Machiavellian glint in his eye that hadn't been there before. If Shiny had picked something up from the house, he wasn't carrying it, so whatever it was had to be small enough to go in his pocket. I tried to come up with a list of murder weapons that might fit the bill, but all I could think of was that scene in The Godfather where wife-beater Carlo Rizzi gets into the front seat of a car, only to be garrotted by Clemenza. It didn't make me feel any better.

'Right. Head for St Mary's.'

'What, the lighthouse?'

'That's the one.'

'We're not goin to the airport, then?'

He let out a low laugh. 'No foolin you, is there bonny lad?' He winked. 'Never tell taxi drivers anything they divvent need to know - they're worse than bloody women for gossip.'

He was right about that. 'So where are we goin, then?'

'Just aim for St Mary's.'

I did as I was told and headed up to the main road and back the way we'd come.

I couldn't imagine why he'd want to go to a lighthouse, but as there'd likely be a few tourists around, it wasn't an obvious spot to commit murder. Or maybe it was a ruse so I would think we were going somewhere safe, when in fact he was just waiting for an opportunity to slip that wire round my neck and drag me over the back, kicking and screaming. Literally.

I kept to the speed limit, hoping a more logical solution would come to mind, but every time I dropped below 40, my passenger reminded me he hadn't got 'all fuckin day'.

I was still worrying about possible murder

techniques when we hit The Links road. Approaching the turn off to the lighthouse, I'd just flicked on the indicator when Glossy Bonce tapped me on the shoulder.

'No, mate. Carry on round the corner.'

I followed the road. On one side was the cemetery and on the other a caravan site. I didn't know which was worse.

'Turn right here.'

I eased the car under the welcoming arch.

Carver Caravans was a sort of mini resort with its own bars and clubhouse as well as an overpriced and under-stocked shop and a down-at-heel arcade. If the punters wanted to, they needn't ever leave the site, though why anyone would come here in the first place was beyond me.

'Round to the left.'

I followed his instructions until we ended up at the far side of the site outside what I assumed was, in caravanning terms, a classic example of top-end accommodation. My experience of caravans was limited to those twenty-foot tin boxes my folks used to foist on me and Jessie every damn year when we spent a fortnight freezing our respective nuts off on the outskirts of Scarborough. This was a different can of crabs altogether - the thing was more like a small house than a touring caravan and it had more gleaming metal on it than a bunch of knights on a crusade.

I stopped the car and Baldy got out. I watched him walk up onto the decking and knock on the door. After a moment, he disappeared inside and I saw him through the window talking to a grey-haired woman who seemed to be wearing a deck chair, or more likely, a gaudy-looking dress. She looked familiar and eventually I remembered who she was.

When I'd first started driving for Ronnie's Taxis we used to get a lot of business down here, but it tailed off after Billy Carver suffered a massive heart attack in the middle of a talent competition. His wife had gamely carried on with the business and it soon transpired that she had a better head for finances than he'd ever had. She bought a minibus and hired a driver so punters wouldn't need to use taxis. Then she extended the clubhouse and added a restaurant to the seaward side, giving those lucky people even more reason to stay put. Though the place was still a bit of a dive, she'd finally got rid of the shittier side of Carver's Holiday Lets.

Watching her through the window, I couldn't imagine Sheila Carver as a crime boss, but I wouldn't bet money on it - I've lost out to women before and I reckoned if they put me up against her, I'd be the one walking home without my shirt.

My hairless friend came to the door and curled a finger at me. I got out the car and followed him into the small house. He stood by the door and waved me towards his leader. I had to admit the place was pretty impressive. There was a walnut cabinet on one side next to a bookcase stuffed with classic crime thrillers. Sheila lounged in a leather chair.

From the look of it, several rare animals had contributed their hides to its creation. Two sour-faced younger guys sat on one of the fitted sofas behind her. From their ages and familial features, I guessed they were the sons.

Everyone was looking at me.

'Ralph tells me you've been helping us out?'

For a woman in her seventies, she sounded as sexy as someone at least three years younger.

'Ralph?' I looked at the sons assuming she meant one of them.

She waved a finger at Cue Ball.

'Oh, aye.' I forced a smile for my new friend. I wasn't sure what she meant by 'helping out', but I definitely didn't appreciate all this attention. If something bad was going to happen, I was in the right place.

'We were all really sorry to hear about Ronnie.'

From her expression, I judged she was either totally sincere or a bloody good liar.

'Aye, me too.'

'He was a good friend to us - especially to my Billy.' She patted a leather pouffe beside her. 'Why don't you sit down?' She clicked her fingers and one of the sons got up and poured drinks.

I lowered myself onto the seat, aware that I was now looking up at Mrs Carver. If it was a deliberate move to put me in a position of vulnerability, it worked - I felt like a kid at primary school, waiting for a spoonful of whatever the equivalent of cod liver oil was at the Carver residence.

The son passed me what looked like a whisky tumbler, but the faint odour wasn't alcoholic.

Sheila grinned and took a sip from her own glass. 'Ginger beer. Never touch booze these days. Not after what it did to my Billy.' She paused and gazed down at me as if deciding what fate to dish up. 'They say Ronnie died in your flat.'

I nodded and glanced at the others. They were all staring at me, though their expressions were too neutral to guess what might be going on in their heads.

She gave me a sly wink. 'I'm assuming it wasn't you?'

'Course it wasn't. What ye think I am?' There was an edge to my voice I hadn't intended, but it seemed to please her.

'Fair enough, and how well d'you know Sven Andersson?'

'I don't.'

'Never met him?'

'No.'

'But you know his...' She hesitated. 'His woman?'

'Only cos I picked her up the other night. I don't know her.' I glanced up at Ralph, but he was gazing out the window.

Sheila shuffled herself round so she was leaning on the arm of the chair. Her face was barely twelve inches from mine and there was a hint of Embassy Regal on her breath.

'Look, Terry...' A purple fingernail reached out and stroked the back of my hand in an Ernst Blofeld sort of way. 'I want to know who killed Ronnie and I think you can help me find out.'

My head was shaking before I could stop it. 'You need to be speakin to the cops. This is nowt to do with me.'

'Oh, but it is to do with you, Terry.' She smiled as if explaining something to a simpleton. 'I have friends in the police force - good friends, but they're not telling me anything and I think it's because they don't know anything. And when the police don't know anything, we have to look elsewhere for answers, wouldn't you agree? Now, you're involved whether you like it or not and whoever killed Ronnie and old Frankie is still out there, and they're looking for something.'

I sat up straight. 'You think Frank was murdered?'

'Don't you think so?'

I shook my head. Shrugged. 'I don't know.'

She leaned back and made a small gesture with her hand. Ralph reached into an inside pocket and produced a bundle of money. He counted out five notes and handed them to me.

I took the cash and looked at Sheila. 'What's this for?'

'Your fare, obviously.'

'There's too much here,' I said, holding the money out to her.

She pushed my hand back. 'Call it a decent tip, Terry. Anyway, we'll be using you again, now we know you're on side.' She smiled in a kindly-grandma way.

I stood up. 'I'm not on anybody's side.' But I knew it didn't matter what I said - I was in the gang and that's all there was to it.

She nodded. 'Don't call us, we'll call you.'

Ralph produced a mobile phone and passed it to me. 'Hot line. Divvent leave it lying around.'

Mrs Carver was grinning. 'Like I said, we'll call you.'

As I climbed back into the car, I heard Carol's voice demanding that I call in. I clicked the mic.

'Car ten clear, Carver's Caravans.'

There was a burst of static then a Carol-type sigh. 'What you doin down there, Terry?'

'Tell ye later.' I glanced back at the caravan. Shiny-head Ralph was standing at the window, watching.

Chapter 6

When I got back to the taxi office, Lizzy was waiting for me.

'Can we talk?'

Feeling a sigh slipping out, I coughed and rubbed my face. 'Sure, why not.' I glanced at Carol, who gave me one of her 'aye, right' looks.

'I'll be back in a minute,' I said.

Lizzy followed me down the stairs and across the road. I walked over to one of the benches the Council provided for old folk and tourists. The sun had warmed the wood enough to take the chill off. I sat down and slid out of my coat, placing it next to me on the bench so Lizzy wouldn't be tempted to sit too close. The tide was coming in and there was a seaweedy smell in the air.

She plonked herself down with a sniff. 'So ye're back on the cars?'

'Aye, well, Ken asked me.'

She gave an almost imperceptible nod. 'I heard about Ronnie.'

'Guessed ye wouldn't have come up to the office if he was still around.' I glanced sideways at her. She looked tired. 'How are you?'

A noncommittal shrug. 'How d'you think?'

'The police been to see you?'

She nodded. 'They're not releasing Frank's body. Not yet.'

I wanted to ask if they were suspicious, but couldn't work out how to frame that sort of question without it sounding like I was accusing her of something. 'D'you know what you're going to do? I mean, afterwards?'

She took a breath and let it out slowly. 'I didn't think it would be like this, you know? Thought I'd be able to cope, an that.' She turned towards me and blinked rapidly, the tears ready to stream down her face.

'I know.' My hand was on hers before I could stop myself. She gripped my fingers and I felt a tremor in her arm.

'Anything I can do?' I said. There it was again - Terry the Shoulder, lean on me and I will give you succour. Or whatever. 'Our Jess was asking after ye.' This wasn't strictly true - my sister's only reference to Lizzy had been something along the lines of 'I suppose that fuckin bitch'll get Frank's house?' I had a vague recollection of the happy couple's reception when an acutely pissed Frank had told me he'd only married Lizzy so she'd always have somewhere to live. At the time I'd thought it was the lager talking, but a few months later, in a more serious moment, he revealed a little more than I wanted to hear.

'No,' she said. 'I'll be fine. Just need to get through it, ye know?'

She was quiet for a minute, then, 'D'you know what happened?'

'How d'you mean?'

'That Friday. Did ye see him at all?'

Perhaps this was Lizzy finally showing her true feelings, wanting to know the details of her husband's final hours, trying to put right what could now never be put right. Or maybe she just didn't want to be implicated in whatever it was Frank had got himself into, if in fact he'd got himself into anything. On that score, I was a long way from sure.

'No,' I said. 'I hadn't seen him for a few days.' It wasn't quite the truth, but it would do for now. If I ever found out the whole story maybe I'd tell her. Then again, maybe I wouldn't.

We sat in silence for a few minutes, then she fastened her coat and stood up. 'I'm going. If ye find out anythin..?'

I nodded. As I watched her walk away, I couldn't help feeling she hadn't said what she'd meant to say.

Carol was standing by the window when I got back to the office.

'What's she got to say for hersel, then?'

'Not a lot, as it happens.' I sat on the counter and turned one of the job sheets round. 'Much happening?'

She sat down. 'That's what I was goin ter ask you.' She inclined her head to one side and gave me a look that told me she wasn't happy. 'What the fuck went on with that job? Supposed to be going to the airport.'

I gave her the bones of the journey with Ralphy

and my invitation into Sheila Carver's boudoir. I left out the bit about thinking I might get garrotted.

That familiar small crease worked its way down her forehead. 'Doesn't make sense. If they're involved with the Andersson lot, who the hell killed Ronnie?'

'Well, we don't know that they're actually involved with Andersson. I mean, it was Elise I took to the Nugent Crescent house. And she obviously wasn't meant to be going there, otherwise that would have been the job from the start.'

'So she changed it?'

I nodded.

'But it must've been her that asked for a taxi in the first place?'

I recalled what Ralph had said about not telling taxi drivers the truth. 'Not necessarily.' I swung my legs round to the other side of the counter so I was facing her. 'Anyway, we don't know who else was at the Hexagon that night.' I had a thought. 'Check the job sheets - maybe one of the guys picked up from there later on. Whoever else was there must have left eventually.'

'Yours was the only account job for Monday night.'

I pulled a face. 'Unless there was another job that wasn't on account.'

'Maybe...' She twisted round and picked up a sheaf of papers off the filing cabinet. Flicking through, she ran a finger down the list of jobs. 'No, nothing else here from the Hexagon.'

'Assuming whoever it was called it in...'

'Nah, it got busy after that and there wouldn't have been time for any of the guys to squeeze in extra jobs.'

I tapped a finger on the sheet. 'You're very trusting.'

She frowned. 'What'd ye mean, like?'

'I mean, if a driver delays calling in when he's picked up, he can also delay when he calls clear.'

She thought about this for a minute, then let out a yelp. 'What? Is that what you do?'

I grinned. 'Course not, but it's easy - provided the extra job is a short one.' I nodded towards Ken's office. 'Ronnie used to do it all the time.'

'Maybe he did, but it was his business. What about the rest of them?'

It was true I didn't feel the same sense of loyalty now as I had when I was a full time driver, but neither did I want to drop anyone in it. 'They all do it occasionally, but it'd make very little difference in terms of actual takings.' I shrugged. 'Chicken feed, really.'

'Might be chicken feed to you, but a percentage of that belongs to the company.'

'What, and you care about that?'

She laughed. 'No, I suppose not. Not really. S'long as I get paid.'

I stood up. 'I'm going back out. Pick you up later, all right?'

I pulled onto the rank behind Fat Barry. There

weren't a lot of punters around so I got out and jumped in next to him.

'Ong ty noh see.' He was munching on a giant Mars Bar and there was a bottle of Coke jammed in-between the seats. If Barry's wife ever found out what he did with the sandwiches she made up for him, he'd be in a shitload of trouble.

'Did ye see Frank on Friday night?'

He shook his head, still munching.

'He must've been on the rank?'

Barry wiped his mouth. 'Course. Didn't talk to him, though.'

Frank had never been a chatterbox, but him and Barry often jumped in each other's cars when it was quiet. So either Frank had had something on his mind, or Barry was talking shite.

'What about Geoff? Wasn't there some hoo-ha down at the Ferryboat?'

'Certainly was - one of the bouncers chucked a couple of the regulars down the steps at the back. Didn't see it maself but Geoff reckoned one of the blokes was a right cockin mess. Needed stitches.'

'Since when have they had bouncers at the Ferryboat?'

'Only the last few weeks. Under new management, ye know? They have bands on at weekends now. Good crowd in there supposedly.' He stuffed the last of the Mars into his mouth.

I stared through the windscreen. There was nothing moving on the rank. 'What about the Hexagon? Ever pick up from there?'

'Nah.'

'What, never?'

He waved a hand evasively. 'I'm usually off by six.'

'D'you know if Frank ever picked up there?'

'Frank? Nah, don't think so.' He'd turned his head so I couldn't see his eyes. Liar, liar, pants on bloody fire. 'Hey up, we're movin.' He started the car and I climbed out, wondering if there was anyone left I could trust.

A few minutes later, I got a fare with a follow-on terminating at North Shields. The drop-off was on Tanners Bank and there was a bit of a snarl-up as I came back along the Fish Quay. It was then I noticed the car: a black Volvo saloon with tinted windows. It slid past me going in the opposite direction. I had the feeling I'd seen it before, but couldn't recall where or when. Instead of nipping up one of the side roads like I'd usually do, I continued on along to New Quay then up Borough Road. The Volvo must have done a quick U-turn for it appeared in my rear-view and followed me up towards the Metro station. I turned onto Rudyerd Street then put my foot down and did a few quick left and right-handers til I was back up on the Tynemouth Road.

The Volvo was nowhere to be seen. In any case, I was probably just being paranoid.

I took my time for the rest of the return journey, mentally listing the things I didn't know and those I might feasibly find out. It struck me I still hadn't seen a photo of Sven Andersson. It also occurred to me where I might get one.

Parking up on Royal Parade, I sat for a few minutes mulling things over. On a nice day, the view overlooking Tynemouth Beach was worth the effort. Today though, the sky was splodged with dark clouds and only a handful of dedicated individuals braved the chill wind in the execution of dog-walking duties.

I didn't bother getting a ticket from the machine - strictly speaking, taxis weren't allowed in public car parks, but there were never any traffic wardens round at this time of the afternoon, so I reckoned it'd be safe enough for half an hour.

The house was a two-minute walk. I rang the bell and walked in, finding my way by following the ever-present aroma of Eau de Vieille Femme.

The old woman in question could usually be found in the living room at the back of the house. As I pushed the door, she was sitting at the dining table by the window, half facing away from me. In front of her a puzzle book lay open, her pen poised, face creased in concentration.

'Left your front door open again, Milly,' I said in a loud voice.

'Ooh, bloody hell.' She jumped visibly and dropped her book on the floor. Twisting round to face me, she waggled a finger. 'Terry, man, ye giv iz such a fright.' She giggled and flung her arms around me. 'Howay an sit yersel doon, lad.'

I took the chair by the fire and waited for her to

settle herself again. 'I can put the kettle on if ye like, Auntie?'

'Why, d'ye want one?'

'No, you're all right - I thought you might.'

She shook her head vigorously. 'Maybe in a minute. Canna drink too much these days. Be running to the bloody lavvy every half hour. Now, what are ye up to? How's that nice young lady of yours?'

'She's not my nice young lady any more.'

'Oh, fer God's sake.' She dropped her head and stared at me over the top of her bifocals. 'Ye haven't been pokin someone else, have ye?'

'Not me.'

She pursed her lips and nodded. 'Ah. Oh well, plenty more kippers on the beach. So what are ye after? Ye've not just come to see me, have ye? Not at this time of day.'

'Actually, no. I was wondering if ye had last week's copy of the Post?'

'Last week? Bit out of date, aren't ye?' She pointed to a pile of newspapers in the coal bucket next to my chair. 'Be one of them, I expect. What ye looking for?'

I leaned down and picked up a handful. The one I wanted was on top. 'Just an article about a bloke I know.'

Unfolding the newspaper, I scanned it carefully and found the article on page five. The heading was *A Wealth of Praise for Swedish Firm* and the story told how businessman Sven Andersson had turned around a small northern company with a huge investment of capital. Apparently, he'd negotiated a deal with local councils for three new blocks of flats. The reporter blabbed on about how the 'handsome Swede' was working with small businesses in the northeast and as well as assisting the housing shortage, had committed to building a number of industrial units. On the right hand side of the story, a photo showed some po-faced councillor shaking hands with a tall blond bloke whose gaze was firmly fixed on the camera.

'Ye found it, pet?'

'Aye, that's it.' I looked at the image again. There was something else about it I couldn't figure out, but my head was too full of other stuff to think about it now. 'Mind if I keep this?'

'Course not, it'll only go on the fire.'

'Thanks Milly.' I tore the article out, folded it up and slipped it into my wallet. 'Now, how about that cup of tea?'

I passed her the Suduko book, then went through to the kitchen to put the kettle on. While I waited, I made a couple of phone calls.

It was just after six when I got back to the office. Ken was leaning against the doorpost watching Carol gather her things together.

I looked at the old man. 'You're not doin the desk tonight, are ye?'

'Might as well. I'll only sit at home doin nothin otherwise. The evenin-shift lads'll be in shortly.' He glanced at Carol. 'So where are yous two goin to be?'

'Not sure yet,' I said. 'I'll text ye later.'

'Aye. Keep yersel's safe.'

Outside it was starting to get dark. There were a few people around, here and there, mostly heading for home. Others stood in pub doorways, wreathed in clouds of cigarette smoke. A few young couples strolled along the Esplanade, and a gang of kids jumped up and down on one of the benches me and Lizzy had sat on earlier. There were no obvious psychos, hockey-stick wielders or men in striped jerseys. But just because I couldn't see them, didn't mean they weren't there.

'Maybe we should stay here? Bring some sleeping bags over, an that?'

Carol stared at me. 'What the fuck for?'

I glanced up at the office window. 'In case they come back.'

She moved her head slowly from side to side. 'Ken's a lovely bloke and that, at least, he is compared to Ronnie, but he's big enough to look after himself. And I divvent want to end up with me face bashed in and a knife in me tits.'

'Aye, I'm sure you're right.'

She gave me one of her looks.

I laughed. 'What?'

'I know you - if we find Ken lying in a pool of blood tomorrow mornin, ye'll be blamin me.'

I took her arm. 'Come on.'

'Where we goin?'

'Somewhere else, that's where.'

We stopped off at mine, then Carol's, picking up essentials and enough supplies for what I hoped would only be a few days. Then, taking a round-about route, I headed for the proposed hideout, doubling back a few times in case we were followed, but unless the bad guys were unbelievably devious, I reckoned we were in the clear.

It was proper dark by the time we arrived. I stopped to pick up the keys then took the anti-clockwise road. Pulling the car up onto the grass verge, I switched everything off and waited for Carol's inevitable reaction.

'You're fuckin jokin, Terry?'

'What's wrong with it?'

'It's a caravan.'

I leaned forward and pointed. 'See that big fancy one down the end there? That's where old Ma Carver lives.'

'And what? Ye think she's goin to protect us?' She wasn't exactly angry but there was a definite tension in her voice.

'Look, it's just somewhere to stay for a few days.'

'And in the meantime you're goin to find out who murdered Ronnie, before some psycho-bastard kills us in our beds?'

'I can take you somewhere else, if ye like?'

She sniffed in a way that suggested she appreciated the gesture, then shook her head. 'If I wake up dead tomorrow, I'll be really annoyed.'

'That your new catchphrase, is it?'

She faked a smile and got out of the car.

While Carol unpacked her things, I did a quick recce of our new abode. There was only one door and the windows were lockable. On the roof was a vent, which, if my expectations of disaster had been particularly high, I might have blocked up, lest some kind of explosive device happened to find its way into our lair. But given that the killer's modus operandi so far related only to knives and hockey sticks, I thought we'd be fine.

I closed the curtains and made myself aware of the location of the nearest weapons (rolling pin, French cook's knife, corkscrew), and set about knocking up a spag bol. Carol checked out the TV and found a few DVDs. I was glad to see she seemed to have calmed down a bit, so while waiting for the spaghetti, I opened a bottle of Pinot Grigio. Relaxing in front of the box was exactly what I needed.

While we waited for the spaghetti, I told Carol about the car with the blacked-out windows, though didn't let on just how worked up about it I was. There was no point in us both being jittery. I thought about showing her the newspaper cutting of Andersson as well, but reckoned she had enough to think about for now.

It was after eleven when Johnny Depp finished putting the world to rights. The wine was gone and

Carol's yawns were getting infectious. She started making moves towards the bedroom. We hadn't discussed sleeping arrangements but since she'd already stashed her things in the only proper bedchamber, it wasn't hard to guess who'd be sleeping on the put-me-up.

There was a moment of awkwardness as we negotiated toilet facilities, then we said our goodnights and Carol disappeared into her room. I sorted my bedding and stretched out for a few minutes, going over everything in my head, but there were still too many unanswered questions. Not feeling as relaxed as I'd expected, I didn't bother getting undressed. My mind sifted through the various pieces of the puzzle that were sliding around in my brain, and at some point over the next half hour, I dozed off.

Something poked me in the chest.
And again.
I opened my eyes.
My first thought was that I couldn't remember switching the lights off. I blinked in the gloom and rubbed my face. As I turned over, I found Carol crouching by my bed, dressed only in skimpy knickers and a t-shirt. Her eyes were wide and she held a quivering finger to her lips.

Her voice was low and her fear was palpable. 'I think there's somebody outside.'

'Fuck.' I scrambled out of bed and pulled my shoes on. 'Ye saw them?' I crept over to the nearest window.

'No, I didn't want to look in case...you know?'

I nodded and carefully lifted one side of the curtain. The orangey glow from the light at the corner of the road seemed unusually vivid. I dropped the curtain and listened. For a moment, there was nothing, then the quietest of thuds, like someone dumping a couple of rubbish bags.

'What is it?' said Carol, her face pale in the darkness.

I tried to focus on where the sound was coming from. Carol started to speak, but went silent as the noise came again. This time is was more defined - something sloshed against the side of the caravan then a whooshing sound came from a spot a few yards from where we stood. I stepped towards the longest window. Carol grabbed my sleeve.

'It's okay.' I held up a finger, silencing her. Stepping carefully, I took hold of the two corners where the curtains met and jerked them open.

It seemed as if the flames leaped upwards right on cue, filling the window with dazzling, orangey light.

'We're on fire!' Scrambling across to the tiny kitchen, I yanked the extinguisher off its hook on the wall, and pulling out the pin, grasped the apparatus firmly in my right hand. In the back of my mind, I was vaguely aware of thudding footsteps, as if someone was running away. I reached for the door key.

'No!' Carol pulled me back. 'What if they're

waiting?'

I dithered for only a moment, but the thought of the pair of us playing the main roles in a human version of barbecued ribs was enough motivation to make up my mind. Unlocking the door, I picked up the rolling pin and pointed at the kitchen knife. 'Grab that.'

'Divvent giv iz a bloody knife - I might stab somebody!'

'Fine.' Yanking the door open, I remembered too late that it would've been sensible to check for heat first. The piles of rubbish against the decking were well alight. As the blaze surged upwards, I jumped back, knocking Carol over. The fire licked around the doorframe, singeing the carpet. In front of us was a wall of flame.

'Water! Get water, quick!' I struggled to my feet as Carol crawled to the sink. Fumbling with the taps, she twisted them feverishly. 'There's nothing coming out.'

'We'll have to jump over it, okay?'

Her lower lip trembled, but she nodded.

We stood there, Carol slightly behind me, bracing ourselves for the ordeal. 'On three - one, two, three!' I cleared the flames easily and fell against the wooden railing at the side of the step, but Carol had caught her shirt on the doorframe and was dragged back inside. Dropping the extinguisher and rolling pin, I jumped over the threshold. Slipping a hand round her waist, I picked her up and leapt back through the flames, landing in a tangle of arms and legs on the grass.

Picking up the extinguisher again, I pulled Carol to her feet and took a few steps backwards. Taking in the scene, I counted six separate fires on this side of the caravan, all strategically placed under windows and around the door. The sheer pace of the inferno as the flames engulfed the entire van was incredible. If we'd left it a few seconds longer we'd have been baked like an overdone Sunday lunch.

I got the extinguisher to work and aimed the spray at the foot of the nearest fire, but whatever fuel our tormentor had used seemed immune to water. The noise of our escape must have disturbed our neighbours, as already several pyjamaed individuals were hurrying towards us with buckets and fire blankets.

Carol was still gripping my arm when Inspector Brown sauntered over to where we stood at the door of one of our neighbours' chalets.

'Can't leave you two alone for a bloody minute, can I?' She turned towards what was left of the blaze. The fire brigade had started packing up their gear while a lone officer picked through the skeletal remains of the black, crispy mess, all that was left of the caravan.

'Wonder the pair of em weren't burnt to a fuckin cinder, if ye ask me.' One of our neighbours, Peggy Jamieson, gave Charis a stern look as if it had been her fault. 'Comin ter summat when folk can't 'ave a bleedin holiday without some arsehole settin fuckin fire to em.' She took Carol's mug off her. 'Want another un, luv?'

Carol nodded and the woman went back inside after giving Charis another hard stare.

'Don't suppose either of you saw anything?'

I shrugged. 'We heard noises, but no. Nothing.'

'Excellent.' She went off to talk to one of the fire officers. Most of the folk who'd been standing round watching were starting to drift away, but a familiar face moved towards us.

'Might have been useful if ye'd let us know yous were here.' He nodded at the remains of our short-stay accommodation. 'Lucky escape, I'd say.' His face was grim and I thought I detected a hint of actual concern in his dark eyes. 'Anyway, Mrs Carver wants to know if you'd like to bunk up at hers.' Ralph Shiny-Head looked at me, then at Carol and back to me.

'That's very kind of her,' I said, 'but I think we'll make our own arrangements. Thanks.'

He nodded and walked away.

'That's the baldy feller ye were on about?' said Carol.

'That's him.'

'Seems like a canny bloke to me.'

'Well, now he does, yeah.'

'So what's next, Mr Ideas man?'

Chapter 7

'Mind, we're not making a habit of this, right?' Charis waggled a finger at me. 'I'm a copper, not a social worker.' She shared out what was left of the bacon between Carol and me, then settled down to eat her toast.

It was eight o'clock in the morning and the kitchen was bright and airy. The view over Jesmond Dene was almost idyllic and it was hard to believe the chaos of the night before had only been a few hours ago. I glanced at Carol who, like me was wearing an old dressing gown, but she was concentrating on her breakfast.

'Ye been here long?'

Charis nodded. 'About six years.'

'Nice place.'

'Aye.'

'Just you, is there?' I tried to make it sound like I was making conversation. Charis looked up.

'Ask a lot of questions, don't ye?'

'Well, until a few days ago, I hadn't seen ye for years, so...'

'My partner died.' She swivelled round in her chair, avoiding eye contact. I wondered if we were talking male or female.

'Sorry. That must've been hard.'

'It was.'

Carol gave me a kick under the table. I stuck my

tongue out at her.

Our host poured more coffee. 'So my DC should be here shortly. I want to go over everything.' She glanced at me. 'And I do mean everything. Whatever it is you're not telling, you can stop that shite right now.'

'We will have to go into work, though,' I said. 'Can't expect Ken to manage.'

'I don't think that's a good idea. If someone's genuinely trying to get rid of the pair of you, there's no reason to think they'll stop just because it's daylight.' She tapped a finger on the table as if thinking it through. 'However, I'm sure Mr Thompson won't object to us hangin on to you for a couple of hours.'

'You're not takin us to the cop shop, then?' Carol sounded relieved.

'Better not. Don't want some fucker burnin the place down.' She grinned.

Charis's office took up the whole of the top floor of the house. There were masses of shelves crammed with police-related textbooks, crime novels and box files. In the centre of the room were two large desks pushed together to form a flat surface, on top of which Charis had laid out a dozen photographs taken after the caravan fire.

Detective Constable Ramshaw struggled up the stairs with a tray of coffee and biscuits. I wondered if he always got the shit jobs. I moved a couple of folders so he could put it down.

Charis stood back and surveyed her handiwork. 'The pictures of the caravan are obviously just those I took last night on my phone, but seein as you were both there, they're not so important.' She leaned forward and picked up one of the images. 'Apart from this one.'

The photo showed a section of grass near one corner of the caravan. 'So this is a possible footprint, and so far, it's the only clue we've got. Not exactly protocol, but I wanted to share this information, otherwise we're never going to work out what's going on.'

'What're these?' I said, indicating the two folders.

'Autopsy reports on Frank and Ronnie.' Charis glanced up. 'You two okay with this?' She was all business. Matter of fact.

We both nodded.

'Right. Frank Armstrong was not murdered. However, we believe he did not die at home. I mean, it's conceivable he might've stretched out and had forty winks on the table and then suffered a heart attack, but I think that's unlikely. The position of the body suggests someone placed him like that. The medical examiner puts time of death at around midnight on Friday, give or take a couple of hours. So he probably died somewhere else.'

'If he wasn't murdered, why bother moving his body?'

'Good point, Mr Bell.' She paused. 'I have my own theories of course, but what do you think?' Her gaze flitted between us.

'Maybe...' I shrugged. 'Maybe he died somewhere...'

'Embarrasin?' Carol was looking at me. 'Like if it was, ye know, in somebody's bed, or somethin?'

Charis leaned on the table. 'How well did you know him? I mean, could he have been having an affair?'

'Don't see how he'd have the time,' said Carol. 'He was workin eight til six most days - and on top of that, he was on Thursday, Friday and Saturday nights til late. You know, two, three o'clock in the mornin, sometimes.'

'Almost as if he didn't want to go home,' said Charis.

DC Ramshaw cleared his throat. We all looked at him. 'According to the work sheets we took from the taxi office, the night he died wasn't particularly busy. At least not for him. He only did ten jobs.'

'That's right.' Charis looked pointedly at Carol.

'Aye, but some of them would've taken a while, like the ones he did on account.'

The inspector exchanged a look with her constable. 'The Andersson account?'

Carol nodded.

'Yes, unfortunately, we can't get hold of Mr Andersson to verify those –'

'But it was Elise Andersson he picked up that night.' From the looks on their faces I realised I'd said this out loud.

'Go on,' said Charis.

I took a breath, then told her about my pickup on

Monday, the conversation with Elise and her sort-of confirmation that Frank had dropped her off.

When I'd finished, Charis glared at me. 'I'll need that address.' She slid her notebook across the table.

'I don't know the number,' I said, scribbling down the street name. 'Though I could find the place again.'

Inspector Brown pulled a face and closed her eyes for a moment. I caught Ramshaw's sly smile before he clocked me watching and resumed his usual deadpan-serious-copper look.

'Anyway,' said Charis, 'according to the log, Frank did two jobs on that account and a couple more over a period of nearly three hours. Why did he only do four jobs? I mean, it was Friday night. Should've been plenty folk about.'

'It depends where he was. If he'd stayed on the rank it'd been busier.' Carol shrugged. 'Sometimes it's just one job after another for all the drivers and they have to do them as quick as they can. Other times, it isn't an issue. Frank might've just sat waitin for the next one to come over the radio.'

I glanced at Carol. 'If he wasn't all that busy and there was nothing on the rank, he probably took a break.'

'There aren't any breaks logged on the sheet for that night,' said Charis. 'Would drivers normally let the person on the desk know?'

I shook my head. 'We're supposed to, especially if we get out the car, but it often doesn't happen. An when it's quiet, it doesn't really matter anyway.'

Charis didn't bother to hide her annoyance. 'Excellent.'

'There's something you haven't mentioned,' I said.

All eyes turned to me. 'About Frank,' I added.

'Go on,' said Charis.

'When I was at his house, on Saturday morning, his car wasn't there.'

The inspector nodded slowly, like she'd been expecting this. 'Yes.' She blinked several times, then, 'Funny you haven't brought that up it before.'

I shrugged. 'Only just thought of it. Anyway, you didn't say anythin.'

Charis folded her arms. 'This isn't a game Terry, ye can't just offer up the occasional fact whenever it pleases you.'

'Huh,' said Carol. 'I didn't think of it either. So is it my fault as well?' She glowered at the police officers, daring them to deny this obvious fact.

'The point is,' Charis went on, 'the car not being there backs up the theory that Frank died somewhere else. When we find the car...' She tailed off.

We continued in this vein for a while longer, then our police pals got an urgent call. I'd brought my car this time, so with Carol still wearing the dressing gown and a pair of Charis's trainers, we headed for the coast.

As I'd not got round to undressing before the fire, I still had my phone and wallet, but most of Carol's belongings had perished in the blaze, including her clothes. As it happened, they weren't the only things to disappear in a puff of smoke - the murder weapon had lain in the bottom on my sports bag for the last few days, so thanks to our arsonistic chum, it'd only be good for charcoal now. Naturally enough, the bag hadn't been the first thing I'd thought of saving when the caravan went up in smoke, and while I was fairly sure the outcome was a good result, the way things had been going, I wouldn't have been surprised if it came back to haunt me.

I was glad the mobile Mrs Carver gave me had been left in the car, where it remained safely unburned. So far, there hadn't been any calls, and though I knew there would be eventually, I hadn't decided yet if I was going to answer them.

We went to Carol's place first. The flat looked the same as when I'd last seen it, but Carol was wary going up the stairs and grasped my hand tightly. She kept me close to her as we peered into each room, then satisfied there were no murderers lurking in the shadows, gathered a few things and shoved them into a rucksack.

'I'll need to ring the bank about my cards an that.'

I nodded and leaned against the doorframe, arms folded. And that's when I remembered the picture of Sven Andersson. I'd stuffed it into my wallet meaning to show it to Carol the night before, but I hadn't wanted her to feel as bombarded as I was with yet more questions. Now, it seemed like it'd be a good idea to pool our resources. Unfolding the paper, I studied it closely, as if the light of a new day might bring it into sharp focus. And perhaps it did, because that's when I realised what had been niggling away at me the day before.

'Goin to yours now, then?'

'Sorry?'

Carol was off the phone. 'I'm sorted,' she said, jiggling her bag. She nodded at the piece of newspaper in my hand. 'What's that?'

I passed it to her. 'Photo of our friend Andersson doing his bit for the community.' I sat on the sofa and watched her face as she studied the image.

'Bloody hell - what a hunk.' She grinned. 'Sorry, that's inappropriate isn't it?'

'Have another look,' I said.

She walked over to the window and stared at the picture. 'What am I looking for?'

'What can you see?'

'Tch, God's sake, Terry, I'm not Doctor fuckin Watson. Gie me a clue.'

'The photo's been cropped, but there's something there you might recognise. Something the photographer couldn't keep out of the image without cutting the legs off his subjects.'

She grumbled a bit, but took another look. 'Like a person, you mean?'

'Not necessarily.'

She peered at it, then her mouth dropped open and she inclined her head. 'Oh.'

I walked over to her and took the photo. It

showed a fenced-off area in front of the half-built apartment block. The photographer must have crammed everyone together on the grass verge by the roadside to get them all in the frame. In the foreground, stood Andersson and the councillor, mostly smiles, with a dozen or so grinning subordinates and the usual community worthies looking on. Behind them was the shell of the building and on the right hand side we could just see the business end of a JCB. On the left side, and slightly in front of the crowd, was the back end of a red Nissan. The licence plate was just visible at the edge of the photo.

It was Frank's car.

I didn't waste any time at my flat - in and out like the SAS, as Sharon used to say on the rare occasions we managed to have sex at the same time.

I'd left Carol in the car and told her to get lost if anyone remotely suspicious showed up. If the place was being watched we'd know soon enough, but there was no way we were serving ourselves up on a platter. The caravan caper had been a bit close for comfort, though I couldn't help but feel we'd managed to stay one jump ahead of our pursuers.

Nevertheless, I was taken aback to find my flat had been done over. The lock was intact, so whoever was responsible hadn't been an amateur. Scattered across the floor, my records, papers and clothes looked like they'd simply been dropped there for effect. I stepped over the mess and checked my one and only hidey-hole. The few important documents I possessed were still there. As there was nothing missing, could this be just another scare tactic? If so, it was working.

One positive point occurred to me as I relocked the front door - the intruders hadn't been clever enough to co-ordinate their visits to coincide with ours. Unless that's exactly the way they wanted it, in which case they probably were clever.

We arrived at Ronnie's Taxis just after eleven. Ken was at the desk. He looked like he hadn't slept for days. There were no punters waiting, only Beardy Bob and Fat Barry who sat with their feet up on the coffee table, reading back-issues of Viz.

'Here he is, ye see,' said Barry, grinning. 'Told ye he wasn't deid.'

'That's not funny,' I said, keeping a straight face.

'Oh, I know, but...' He coughed. 'Just havin a laugh an that, ye knaa?'

Carol made a beeline for the desk. 'Come on you, get yerself away home. We'll take over now.'

Ken sighed. 'Not much to take over, to be honest, pet.' He shook his head. 'Punters are staying away.'

Beardy Bob nodded in agreement. 'It's true. I was on the fuckin rank for nearly two fuckin hours this mornin and not a fuckin soul got in me fuckin car.' He wiped a sleeve across his mouth. 'Not a soul.'

Carol slammed her hand down on the desk. 'Well ye'll not get anythin sat in here ye great lazy sod.'

'I was just sayin.' Bob pushed out his lower lip and stood up. 'Fine, I'll fuck off then.'

Carol slid a finger down the job list. 'There's a pickup from the airport at half two.' She looked up. 'Who was in first?'

Fat Barry pointed at Bob.

'There ye go, then.' She scribbled the address on a slip of paper and held it out. Bob sniffed and took it.

'Go on, it'll take ye half an hour to get over there. And this time don't forget to take a bit of card with the bloke's name on. Don't want Coastal nicking our customers again.'

He nodded solemnly and went out.

I'd not moved from third car on the rank for nearly an hour when I saw her. She was heading for Paedophile Pete in the white Vauxhall and already had her hand on the door when she caught sight of me.

Now, according to Taxi-Driver Law, customers are expected to take the first car they come to on a taxi rank, irrespective of which firm it belongs to, so strictly speaking Elise Andersson should have jumped in with Pete, but when our eyes met, she shut his door and walked towards my car.

Paedo boy was out of the car in a second. I wound my window down ready for the blitz of bad breath.

'Er sorry missus but you have to take the first one.' He pointed to the Vauxhall and shrugged like it wasn't his fault.

Elise opened my rear passenger door. 'But I like this one.'

'No, seriously, ye have to get in the first car, an that.' He glared down at me. 'Come on, Terry, ye know how it works.' His voice was much like his face - whiny and thin.

'You got an account with SAHB then?' I said, holding back a smile.

He crouched down and looked over at Elise who was now sitting in the back, her face all innocence. 'Well, no, but...'

I shrugged and started the engine. 'No point you taking her, then. Is there? Unless you want to do it free of charge?'

'Did I get you into trouble?' Elise turned and waved at Pete as we pulled out of the line. She looked a little different from our previous meeting. Black trousers and a dark green blouse suited her just as well though, and from the size of the bomber jacket that graced her shoulders, I guessed she'd borrowed it from a Swedish giant.

'No. He was right though, you should've gone with him.'

'But I didn't.'

'So is this on account, then?'

'I thought you preferred cash?'

'I do.'

Her smile lit up my rear-view mirror. 'Whatever suits you.'

I'd reached the end of the one-way bit and pulled up behind a bus at the junction, at which point I realised I hadn't asked where she wanted to go. 'So where you off to?'

'The Hexagon.'

'Bit late for lunch, isn't it?' I tried to sound conversational, but I caught her sharp look in the mirror.

'Did I say I was hungry?' Her tone was a little accusatory.

'I just meant –'

'You were prying, I think.' She laughed but the look was still there. 'Maybe you'd prefer to take me home?'

'And where's that?'

'Not around here.' She turned and gazed out the window. 'We have a place out of town. The countryside, you know?'

'Sounds lovely.'

I keyed the mic and called the job in then headed along the Esplanade. Elise fiddled with her handbag, checking her makeup, running a hand through her hair.

I pulled into the car park at the Hex and checked the meter. 'Five forty, please.'

She handed me a tenner and I made a show of putting it in my wallet and rooting about in my cash bag, hoping she'd say keep the change. But she didn't. When I passed the coins over, she checked the amount and dropped them in her purse.

I watched her climb out and walk up to the door where I'd first set eyes on her. The apron guy appeared from nowhere and opened it, standing aside while she slid past him. I saw her move through the bar area then lost sight of her as a sea of bobbing heads surged out of the main restaurant.

I picked up the mic. 'Car ten clear the Hex.'

Carol must have been waiting for me to call. 'Was that who I think it was, Terry?'

'Who d'you think it was?'

'Don't be funny. Are you free?'

A couple of lumberjacks in denims had disgorged from the back door of the restaurant and were heading towards the car. 'Hang on,' I said into the mic. 'Might have a fare.' One of the guys opened the door and stuck a foot inside, claiming his ride. His friend, whose face bore not a little resemblance to a welded bench, grabbed his arm and said something I didn't hear, then both of them climbed in.

'Where to, lads?'

Something cold and hard jabbed into my neck.

'Just drive, or ye'll get it.'

Chapter 8

'Drive,' the voice said again, its tone low and throaty, reminding me of that bloke who does the voiceover trailers for American movies. In this case, the tag line wasn't promising.

I couldn't tell if the cold, hard thing was a gun. For a couple of seconds I pondered on the wisdom of testing a theory, but guessed there wouldn't be a lot of space for wrong answers. As I turned the wheel in a long arc out of the car park, I saw Apron Man watching us. The look on his face told me that out of the both of us, he thought he had a better chance of getting home that night.

Pulling out onto the main drag, I headed towards Tynemouth. As neither of my passengers objected, I assumed either this was exactly the direction they wanted to go in, or it didn't matter a fuck where we went. I chose to go with the first option.

Taking surreptitious glances at my abductors, I reckoned they couldn't be much older than mid-twenties. There was a spotty-teenager look about them and their clothes weren't exactly Savile Row.

The one sporting the weapon and the least ugly mug lowered his hand. 'Do as ye're told and ye'll not get hurt.'

A quick glance in the mirror suggested this advice was almost certainly bollocks - these guys weren't looking to party. They'd been given a job and nothing was going to stop them. I had to do something, and I had to do it fast.

'I need to call in,' I said, pointing at the radio.

'No you don't,' said Bench Face.

'No, really I do, otherwise the lass on the desk'll know something's wrong.' I caught the quick exchange of views and after a moment, Mr Bench nodded. 'Go on, then, but watch what ye say, or I'll put a fuckin hole in yer, right?'

I cleared my throat. 'I could say I'll be out the car for a while?'

Bench Face grunted. 'Fine.'

I keyed the mic and took a little more care over my diction than usual. 'Car nine, out of the car for a few minutes.'

There was a pause, then Carol's voice came back, 'Was that you, Terry?'

'It was,' I said.

Her reply was swift and casual. 'That's car nine out of the car at the Hexagon.'

We drove in silence for several minutes, then as th ruins of the Priory loomed ahead of us, Gun Man leaned forward. 'Just keep to the main road. I'll tell yer when to turn off.'

Normally, I'd have had half an ear on the radio and be able to follow roughly where other drivers were calling clear. But since picking Elise up, I hadn't been listening, so had no idea if there was anyone nearby. If there was, and we stayed on this road for a while longer, there might be a chance. If there wasn't, I was going to get screwed. And not in a nice way.

Bench Face gazed out the window like he was looking for something. And he wasn't the only one - keeping my head facing forward, I casually clocked each side road as we passed, checking mirrors, hoping for a miracle.

'Watch yer speed,' said the better-looking one.

'Sorry,' I muttered, glad of the opportunity to apply the brakes without it looking suspicious.

Then I saw it - half a block ahead, the hint of a familiar bumper. A bonnet appeared as a pale green Nissan Crappy nosed around a corner. I caught a glimpse of Jimmy Walton behind the wheel. As we sailed past, he swung out and pulled in behind me and for the first time in my life, I was actually glad to see the miserable bugger. However, he was only one and I'd be needing more than that to escape this situation.

Half a mile up the road, my salvation arrived. Joe Spud (metallic grey), appeared on the horizon. Joe was nuttier than a nut cake with extra nuts. He'd been known to employ his particular brand of persuasion in a variety of situations, such as when punters disagreed about the fare. Joe's normally smiley and open face tended to work to his advantage, creating the element of surprise. He'd once ended an animated discussion by bringing his forehead into sharp contact with the nose of his antagonist - a lorry driver who'd erroneously parked his HGV on the taxi rank.

In this case though, Joe's reaction was anyone's

guess.

His car was about thirty yards ahead, with Jimmy right up behind me. Keeping my eyes on Joe, I took my foot off the accelerator and jumped on the brakes. At the same instant, as if we'd planned it that way, Joe's car skidded to a halt, before slewing across my lane, blocking the road. He squealed to a stop a few feet in front of my car.

'What the fuck —' said Bench, but I was already out of the car. Jimmy thudded to a halt, missing my rear bumper by inches, while Joe marched to my nearside passenger door, a large hammer in his right hand.

Bench Face scrambled out onto the pavement just as Joe swung his arm downwards, catching the unfortunate moron a hefty whack in what Joe liked to call 'the pods'. Bench doubled up on the ground, his face taking on a nice shade of purple.

I turned to see where the other man had gone, but the gutless git was already halfway down the road, sprinting like an Olympian desperate for the toilet. Clearly, he'd judged the odds to be against him.

Joe pressed the heel of his boot into Bench Face's left hand and ground it around like he was making coffee.

A quick check inside the car confirmed there was no sign of the gun. Shutting the door, I knelt down beside the squirming mass on the pavement. 'Who sent you?'

The man urged me to go away in words of one

syllable. I looked up at Joe.

'My mate asked ye a question.' He swung the hammer menacingly. 'Ye want to answer? Or will Ah give ye a DIY panel beat and a re-spray?'

'A what?' It was more of a squeal than a reply, but Joe gave him a gentle whack on the shoulder to dispel any lingering doubt about the nature of the panel beat.

'All right, for fuck's sake.'

Joe stepped away, but kept the hammer within bashing distance. Jimmy took up residence behind the man as the whimpering fool struggled to his knees.

'Ah divvent knaa who it was. Honest, Ah divvent.' His face had sagged into a quivering blob. 'Just somebody that giv iz fifty quid to knock ye aboot an that.'

'An what somebody would that be?' I said.

He shrugged, then winced at the pain in his shoulder. 'Nae idea. Honest.'

Jimmy held out his phone. 'Think ye'd better call the cops, eh?'

Bench Face shook his head. 'No, no, divvent dae that - he'll kill iz.'

Joe tapped him on the shoulder again. 'Who will?'

The man shook his head. 'Seriously man, I divvent knaa anythin.'

Joe looked at me. 'What d'you think?'

'Doesn't matter - reckon I know who it is anyway.' I patted Joe on the back. He glanced at my hand like I'd invaded his privacy.

'Aye, well, thanks mate. Much appreciated.'

He nodded. 'Any time.' He gave Bench Face another not-so-gentle tap on the shoulder before going back to his car.

It was only then that I noticed the folks standing round watching us. A few vehicles had stopped, but as Joe's car pulled away, we were no longer blocking the street. Several cars crawled past, ogling the man who was now leaning against the car, nursing his shoulder. The proliferation of mobile phones pointed in our direction told me celebrity status wasn't far away.

Jimmy laughed. 'Be on Facebook afore ye know it.'

I watched Bench Face straighten up. He glared at me and hobbled away, clutching his hurty parts.

'I think ye'd better tell Inspector Brown.'

I was sitting on the edge of the counter back at the office. 'Maybe.'

'Never mind bloody maybe,' muttered Carol. 'It's not just *your* neck we're talking about here, ye know?'

'Aye, I know.'

As if on cue, my phone rang. It was Charis. I gave her the lowdown on recent events. She wasn't as interested as I'd expected and didn't think my theory on who Mr Big was had any merit. Even so, she suggested me and Carol get out of town for a few days. I told her it was a good idea. I may have given her the impression it was such a good idea me and Carol were going to do exactly that, but I didn't tell her what we were actually going to do. In fact, I didn't even tell Carol.

I squared things with Ken and told my running mate I'd pick her up at six. That left me a couple of hours to check something out.

Chapter 9

Stanley 'Bummer' Harris leaned back against the counter and gave me a sly smile. The years had not been kind to him but he still had the slim build I remembered from school sports days. He adopted the hand-on-hip pose usually reserved for his more familiar customers and trotted out his catchphrase: 'So ye've finally come ower to the dark side, have ye?' He grinned salaciously - an expression that always prompted me to clear my throat in a manly way.

'You're not funny, mate.' I sidled across to the rack of fishing rods displayed against one wall and made like I was interested.

'Yes I am, actually,' he cackled, 'and divvent start fingering the goods if ye're not buying.'

'I am buying, but it isn't fish I'm after catchin.'

The grin vanished and his mouth dropped open. He nodded slowly. 'This to do with those murders, is it?' He skipped over to the shop door and shut it firmly. 'I was tellin Mikey the other day - I says Terry Bell wouldn't hurt a fly but I bet he knows more than he's saying. An ye know what Mikey says?'

'I can't imagine,' I said, with no hint of eagerness.

'He says it's the quiet ones ye've got to watch for.' He nodded again.

'Well ye can tell Mikey I haven't murdered

anyone. Yet.'

Harris flapped his hand and guffawed. 'Ooh, stop it!'

I glanced at the window then back at Harris. 'Do ye still keep those...erm...ye know? From when we were kids?'

His tongue slid over his lower lip. 'The er...' He pointed a finger at me and clicked his tongue, then jerking his head towards the back of the shop, said, 'The under-the-counter stuff?'

I nodded.

He put a hand on my shoulder and led me towards the back room. 'Obviously, I don't sell stuff like that, not officially, but if I can accommodate ye, I will. What exactly are ye lookin for?'

When I'd picked out what I wanted, Harris faffed around for a couple of minutes wrapping it up in a bin bag. While he was busy, I perused his selection of what he liked to call 'new psychoactive substances'.

'Not wantin anythin else, are ye, bonny lad? Somethin for the weekend, maybe?' He half turned away and added, in a casual tone, 'I hear your lass walked out?'

'Christ, is nothin sacred?'

'If you're needin a pick-me-up, I know a few folk. Could put ye in touch with someone...suitable?'

'Oh aye? A night of passion followed by a dose of somethin nasty? Not my cup of coffee, Stan.' Then I had another thought. 'Unless...ye don't know a guy called Sven Andersson, do ye?'

He shrugged. 'Nah. Except that he's got big fuck-off car.' Qualifying this, he added, 'Mikey cuts his hair for im.'

I looked at him with renewed interest. 'Really? What sort of big fuck-off car?'

'White BMW.' He giggled. 'Well, not all white - apparently one of his ex-workers chucked paint stripper over the bonnet so it looks a bit of a mess just now.'

'Noticeable, is it?'

'Oh, aye. See it a bloody mile off. So Mikey says.' He gave me a sly wink. 'Why are *you* interested?'

I handed over the cash and took my purchase. 'If I'm still alive at Christmas, I'll tell ye's all about it. Say hello to Mikey for me.'

The back end of the Hexagon stuck out over the promenade, propped up on stilts like some kind of War of the Worlds tripody-type thing. Not having been down on this stretch of the beach for a few years, I hadn't seen the place from this angle before. Admittedly, it was only twenty feet above my head, but the supporting structure looked anything but safe, and I had no wish to be hanging around underneath if the whole thing decided to give in to gravity and hit the sand.

I turned and walked down to the water's edge and pulled out my secret weapon. Not being a fan of bird watching, I'd had little need for a pair of binoculars during my youth, but this pair had turned up when me and Jess were going through our dad's things. I suspected he'd only used them for spying on the neighbours, but these bad boys were particularly high quality so would be perfect for what I wanted.

When I was far enough away so's not to attract attention from diners in the restaurant, I fiddled with the focus until it offered a decent view of the floor-to-ceiling windows in what I assumed was the 'posh' bit of the Hex. Though I'd never eaten there myself, I'd been in the bar a few times and enjoyed a few sneaky peeks of the town's professed movers and shakers while they scoffed foie gras and other equally deplorable foodstuffs.

The view was better than I'd hoped for and I could easily make out the faces of most of the diners in the prime seats. Course, it was only five-thirty so the only people in the place were the early-evening pre-theatre lot, who'd fill their faces before popping over to the cinema or into Newcastle for a northern version of one of the London shows. As expected, the bods I was looking for weren't around, but I'd found what I needed to know, so there was only one more thing to do before picking Carol up.

'I wish ye'd tell iz where we're goin, Terry.' Carol sighed for the umpteenth time.

'See when we get there.'

'Aye, so ye said, but I'm none the bloody wiser, am I?'

It'd been cloudy and overcast all day and by the

time we'd negotiated the city centre, I was pleased to see it was dark enough for what I had in mind. I just hoped my memory of the street matched up with the reality, or it'd be a waste of time.

As we passed Central Station, the profusion of street lighting afforded me a glimpse of what might have been the Volvo with the tinted windows. It was two cars back and followed us for a couple of minutes before I lost sight of it, though as I negotiated the badly-lit areas of the West End, I'd've been hard pushed to say whether the car itself was black, blue or pea-green. In any case, it had gone when we turned into Nugent Crescent.

Keeping an eye out for the green door, I slowed down as we drew level with the dwelling I was interested in. Pulling almost to a stop, I peered across at the buildings to my right. Sure enough, separating each pair of terraced houses, a narrow alley ran from front to back, like a sort of tunnel underneath the upper storeys.

Continuing down to the bottom of the road, I turned the car around and scooted back out onto the main drag, parking up in the same place as last time.

Carol had gone quiet, but it was obvious from the stern looks she was throwing my way she'd sussed what I was up to. Thankfully, she didn't say anything as we walked back down the street. I hoped she wouldn't be tempted to chuck a spanner in my plans.

By chance, the streetlamp beside the alley I was

aiming for wasn't working, giving the immediate area a nicely gloomy outlook. I took a quick look round then grabbed Carol's hand and yanked her down the passageway. It ran between the houses, down to a pair of high wooden gates at the end that joined at a forty-five degree angle. The gates led to the back yards of the houses on either side, though both were in darkness. I pulled Carol in close and made shushing noises.

'Eeh Terry, if ye'd wanted a shag ye should've said - we could've gone to my place.' She gave me a look that confirmed this was a joke.

I leaned against the wall and peered back towards the street. The house with the green door was almost directly opposite and I could see a bit of the front window as well, which was a bonus.

'Stay here.' I walked back to the street and looked down the alley. If I concentrated, I could just about make out a human shape, but unless someone was specially looking for us, we'd be harder to see than a black cat in a coal cellar.

'What'll we do if one of the owner's comes out?'

I shrugged. 'I'll tell them we were looking for a place to have a knee-trembler.'

'By God, ye're a romantic fucker, I'll say that.' She fastened her coat up and dug her hands into her pockets. 'I suppose I'm expected to hang around until ye've seen whatever it is ye're wantin to see?'

'That's the plan.' I moved in beside her and slipped a hand around her shoulders. 'For appearances sake, ye understand.'

'Aye, well, as long as ye realise I'm not goin to be droppin me knickers for appearances sake.'

We'd been stood there for almost an hour before anything happened. Several people walked past, but no-one showed any interest in our hiding place. Then a white car pulled up outside Mr Ahmed's front door. From the way the driver behaved, I assumed it was a private hire vehicle, but there was nothing to show which firm it was from.

Two young women got out the back, giggling and tipsy. By the time they reached the front door, it had opened, and a familiar hairless bonce appeared silhouetted against the hall light.

'Here,' whispered Carol. 'Is that whatsisname?'

'Ralph, yes.' I narrowed my eyes as if that would somehow bring his features into focus. 'At least, I think it is.' I really needed to get closer but even my binoculars wouldn't allow me to see through doors.

When the front door closed and the car had moved off, I turned to look at my companion. In the gloom, her face was almost invisible, but I could feel her warm breath on my neck. I suddenly realised I'd been dragging Carol round like we were joined at the hip, and apart from the occasional moan, she'd gone along with all my decisions, good or bad. Perhaps, for all her jokey denials, she was interested in me after all? However, I reckoned it was more likely she didn't want to be left to her own devices with a killer on the loose.

I glanced back along to the house. I was starting to feel that my current plan was worthless - there we were, standing around in the cold as if we had nothing better to do. What had I expected to see from this spectacularly limited viewpoint? While I had to admit I enjoyed hanging around with Carol, even when I was freezing my nuts off, this was getting us nowhere. We had to make something happen.

'Come on,' I said taking her hand. 'We're going in.'

I started forward, but she pulled me back.

'Going in where?'

'In there.' I pointed to the green door.

'We're bloody not,' she said. 'Not a bloody chance.'

'Look, I just want to knock on the door, then we'll make out we're at the wrong house, or summat.'

'And what if Ralph answers it?'

'Ah, now...' I reached into my inside pocket. 'Luckily, I brought protection.'

Two minutes later, we were standing outside the front door, Carol's fingernails digging into my hand. I could feel my heart banging away like a demented kettledrum in my chest. I prised her fingers away from mine and persuaded her to hang onto my coat. Pressing the bell, I told myself it'd be fine.

The door swung open and a familiar, yet not so familiar, face hove into view.

'Aye, what yer want?'

'We're here for the party?' I said, trying out my upward inflection. My forced smile was almost sincere, but of course he couldn't see it because of the mask.

'Think you got the wrong hoose, mate.' The big baldy bloke started to close the door, when a slim black woman in a blue dress appeared behind him.

'C'mon Horse, I get you another drink, yes?' She glanced at me and then at Carol. 'Who are these people - they think perhaps it is Halloween?' She giggled and disappeared down the corridor.

'Sorry,' I muttered. 'Must be the next street.' I turned Carol around and pushed her up the path.

'Ang on. Ah've seen ye somewhere before, haven't Ah?'

I glanced over my shoulder. 'No, don't think so. Sorry.' Behind the baldy bloke, I caught sight of another familiar face, waving his head around like he was listening to some muted reggae beat, my Jamaican friend didn't seem remotely concerned about his close proximity to the man called Horse. Another one to cross off my list of trusted pals.

Grabbing Carol's hand, I dragged her along the street towards the main road and safety.

Back in the car, I sat staring down at the face of Frankenstein's monster.

'Still don't see why I had to be Ronald Reagan,' said Carol, waving the rubber mask in my face.

'It was all I could get, all right? Anyway, it did the trick.'

'So who was that bloke?'

I shook my head. 'I dunno. Somebody who looks

like Ralph.'

'So if the man you saw on that first night, the one you thought was Ralph...' She paused, a crease running along her forehead. 'If that wasn't him, then it obviously never has been him, so we don't have any reason to think Ralph is involved, do we?'

'No, we don't.'

I was confused. All this time I'd been convinced big Ralphy must have feet planted in both camps. That he had to be the double agent, the traitor, the Tessio to my Michael Corleone. Except, obviously, he wasn't.

'Terry, why did she call him Horse?'

I looked at her. 'You don't want to know.'

Our second stop of the evening was back at the beach. This time we didn't need the masks. I'd forgotten the tide would be in so we were a good deal nearer the overhanging lip of the Hexagon than I'd intended. But it didn't matter - I'd still be able to see what I wanted to see.

'What are we looking for?' Carol's voice had begun to get a bit whiny, like a child who'd dropped her ice-cream on the sand.

'The Anderssons.'

'What makes you think they'll be here?' She waved a hand around dismissively. 'We might be stood here all bloody night for nowt.'

I lifted the binoculars. 'They'll be here.' Adjusting the focus, I scanned along the crowd of diners in the window seats. There was nothing of interest at first, just the usual shmoozers, but then I noticed an empty table in what I took to be the prime spot in the corner of the restaurant. A waiter led two people to the table, taking a few minutes to seat and fawn over them until he was dismissed with a wave of a Swedish hand.

Sven Andersson.

Elise was wearing the same dress she'd worn the first night I saw her. Looking at her through the glasses gave her face a queer sort of flat, two-dimensional appearance, but even so, it was clear from her expression she wasn't happy. I should've asked Bummer Harris if he had any listening devices, though maybe that was going a bit too far.

'Well?' Carol tugged at my sleeve. 'Is it them?'

I handed her the binoculars. 'Have a look.'

'Ah-ha,' she said. 'So what now?'

'Now, we wait.'

'What - again?'

It was almost an hour and a half later that our Swedish friends decided to make a move. I'd given Carol my jacket to stop her moaning about the cold, so my nether regions were getting a bit close to the brass monkey department. Rubbing my hands, I took another look at the Hexagon and was glad to see that finally something was happening.

'Right, that's them going.' I forced the binocs back into their case and grabbing my mobile, sent a text confirming the set-up I'd arranged a couple of hours earlier. I took Carol's hand. 'C'mon.'

We'd left the car on the corner opposite the entrance to the Hex. Just as the engine thrummed into life, twenty yards away a white Beemer with a distinctively shitty-coloured bonnet, slid out onto the road, heading south towards Tynemouth. Quarter of a mile further along, a grey saloon pulled out of its parking space.

'You're not going to follow them?' whined Carol, her hands jammed into her armpits.

'Course. What else would I be doin?'

'An what happens when they get to where they're goin?' I didn't respond straight away so she slapped me on the shoulder. 'I said...'

'I heard.' Glancing in my side mirror I noticed a car behind was flashing its lights. Easing my foot off the accelerator, I swerved nearer the kerb and watched as the blue Rover roared past.

'Shite.'

'What?'

I nodded to the vehicle that was now in front. 'Charis Brown.'

She leaned forward. 'What, in that car?'

'Yes, in that car.' I dropped back just enough to keep the Beemer in sight, while allowing our law enforcement friends plenty of room.

'D'ye think they're followin Andersson as well?'

I shook my head. 'Who knows?'

'D'ye think she saw us?'

'She's a cop. Course she bloody saw us.'

As if on cue, the Rover flashed its fog lights and began to slow, indicating left. An arm appeared out of the passenger side window, making pointing motions. I did as I was told and pulled in behind them.

Watching the Beemer sail off into the distance, I buzzed the window down.

Charis sauntered up like she had all the time in the world. 'Well, well,' she said, crouching down next to the door. 'Out for a drive, eh?' She winked at Carol.

'We were just heading home.'

Her features transformed into an exaggerated frown. 'But surely you both live in the opposite direction?'

'Well obviously we're not staying at our own places, are we? In case somebody tries to kill us. Again.'

'So where are ye staying?' She said. 'Just in case somebody tries to kill ye.'

I sighed. 'The Holiday Inn.'

She sucked in her cheeks and tutted. 'That den of iniquity?' Inclining her head so she could eyeball Carol, she whispered, 'Double room, is it?'

'Look,' I started, but she held up a hand and her range of comedy expressions vanished.

'No, you look. I don't want you anywhere near Sven Andersson. We've checked him out, and her, and we've eliminated them from our enquiries, so I don't want you sticking your binoculars anywhere near, okay?'

She walked back to the car and as she climbed into the driver's seat, the courtesy light lit up DC

Ramshaw's face. He was grinning like the proverbial cat.

Charis heaved a U-turn and sped off back the way she'd come. I waited til they were a blip on the horizon, then slipped into gear and set off after my quarry.

'Cheeky cow,' said Carol. 'Makin insinuations.' She emitted a snorting noise. 'I've a good mind to jump your bones just to spite her.'

'Don't let me stop you,' I muttered.

She laughed. 'You'll be lucky.' She was quiet for a moment then, 'We're not really going to The Holiday Inn, are we?'

'That shithole? Course not. But I still want to find out where Andersson lives.'

She rested a hand on my arm and squeezed it gently. 'Terry, maybe we should just forget it? Leave it to the cops?'

'I would if I thought they were gettin anywhere.'

'Well, unless you've got an Andersson-tracking-device down your pants, we're not likely to find them tonight, are we?'

I pulled up at a mini-roundabout and grinned at her. 'Wanna bet?'

It'd only been a few minutes since the Beemer disappeared so I reckoned they'd have zipped along the seafront and be round the corner into Front Street by now - and that's exactly where I wanted them. As the road bends round, it splits into two, allowing space for a generous parking area that cuts straight down the middle between the carriageways. Even at the best of times, it could be a bit of a gridlock situation and at this time of night, the half-mile or so up to the junction of Tynemouth Road would be chock full of partygoers and the like. Nevertheless, I couldn't bank on Andersson getting caught in the usual snarl-up, so I'd taken the precaution of having a couple of mates on standby.

As we rounded the corner, I spied the Beemer a hundred yards up the road. It wasn't moving.

'What?' Carol stared at me. 'How did that happen?'

I chuckled. Joe's car was parked across the lane, blocking Andersson's progress. The Swede himself was out of his car shouting Scandinavian obscenities in Joe's direction. I hoped my bolshie pal wouldn't rise to the bait and smack him one, but thankfully, as soon as he clocked our arrival, he shunted backwards onto the pavement, pulled forwards and sped away.

'You arranged that?' There was a hint of admiration in her voice.

'I did.'

'How'd you know he'd come this way?'

'I didn't. Geoff was ready to pull a similar stunt if they'd gone the other way.' The set-up had cost me a hundred quid but I reasoned if it helped track down Ronnie's killer, it was money well spent.

She nodded. 'That's quite clever, Terry. For you.'

We followed Andersson up to the junction where he turned left and put his foot down. I had to drop a gear to keep up. A mile further on, he swung a left into Stephenson Street then right onto the A187. As we made the turn, I noticed another car behind us. I glanced at it a couple of times, but reasoned it was pretty unlikely there'd be yet another car following us. Even so, I kept an eye on it until it dropped back out of sight.

'I bet I know where he's going,' said Carol. 'Royal Quays. That's where all the posh folk live.'

'Just cos it's where *you* want to live, doesn't mean it's posh.'

She thumped my arm. 'Like you'd know.'

As it turned out, she was right, though it wasn't the houses Andersson was heading for. We followed the Beemer down through the housing development, over the bridge and onto the road that led to the river. Then we swung left towards the marina and I dropped back, allowing him plenty of space. To the right, the Tyne looked sleek and black and I suddenly felt vulnerable on this narrow stretch of road between two bodies of water. The lights from the boats in the harbour were warm and welcoming, but I didn't imagine Andersson would be happy to see me.

As he swerved into the car park, I took my time negotiating the dead-end roundabout, before doubling back and pulling over.

'Where ye goin, man?' Hissed Carol, as I jumped out.

I signalled she should stay in the car, then skipped over the grass verge separating the road from the marina's parking areas and hurried across to the edge of the quay. I could still see the Beemer moving slowly along the far side and a moment later, it backed into a space.

Crouching down, I watched Andersson get out the car and go to the boot, though whatever he took from it up must have been small. I tried to imagine what it might be - something small that you'd want to keep in the boot. Something valuable, maybe? Or something dangerous.

My line of thought was interrupted as Carol came up beside me. Except, unless she'd taken to wearing black overalls and started smelling of fish, it wasn't Carol.

I looked up. 'Ah, hello.'

Bench Face grinned down at me. 'Hiya.'

I straightened up slowly and glanced over at the car. Carol's face appeared distorted, held hard against the rear passenger window. A man sporting an amount of facial hair that would've looked indulgent on an ape, had a hand around her mouth.

Mr Face jabbed a cold, hard object into my side. This time, I didn't bother speculating on what it might be. Grabbing my arm, he marched me back to the road.

Monkey Boy leaned over and opened the rear passenger door, then shifted over to the other side, taking Carol with him. That left Carol in the middle and me stuck behind the driver's seat. Bench kept the gun on me until I'd shut the door. Hairy-Face had his hand around Carol's neck. He was big in the shoulder department and I could see it wouldn't take much effort for him to do her serious damage. As his pal climbed into the driving seat, I found myself wondering where their car was. If they'd already been here when we arrived, they couldn't have known we were coming, and if not, where'd they sprung from? Remembering the car I'd seen earlier, I guessed I should've taken more notice of my rear-view mirror. In any case, it wasn't something I needed to spend time worrying about just now.

Mr Bench pushed his seat back, squashing my knees. The comfort of prisoners wasn't on his list of priorities. He leaned over and passed the gun to his hirsute friend.

'Where's your pal tonight?' I quipped. 'Out eating children?'

'Yer sense of humour's a bit like your pal Ronnie's,' said Benchy, starting the car. 'So ye'll be glad to know ye'll be meetin up with him soon.' He laughed heartily as the car pulled away.

Chapter 10

It came to mind that as we were leaving the vicinity of Mr Andersson, we obviously weren't being taken to see him. Although, with his goody-three-shoes clean-cut image, it might be fair to assume he wouldn't want dead bodies cluttering up his nice posh yacht. No, he almost certainly had a derelict warehouse somewhere for jobs like this. Somewhere out of the way, where trivial matters like spilled blood and murder could be dealt with quietly.

There was another possibility of course, that I was mistaken about Andersson and it was this Ahmed bloke who was pulling the strings, but even though the gorgeous Elise knew the guy, I'd been wrong about Ralph being one of his cronies, so now the odds didn't seem so strong. Then again, we were already on the coast road heading for Newcastle, so maybe Ahmed and his horsey friend were already waiting for us.

As it turned out, I was right about one thing - we'd been driving for ten minutes when we turned onto the A19, then took a series of right and left-handers along roads that were markedly deficient in signage. In the dark, I wasn't certain where we were, but the lack of streetlights suggested our destination to be The Middle of Bloody Nowhere.

Minutes later, we were thumping along a rough track that was so full of potholes, our heads banged with annoying regularity against the roof of the car. With Hairy-Face at a disadvantage because of the colossal size of his skull, he was momentarily distracted, so I took the opportunity to reach under the driver's seat and cop hold of my spanner. Glancing at Carol I realized she'd seen what I was up to and had shuffled herself forward to distract her captor's attention. Trouble is, now I had this great big spanner and nowhere to hide it. I knew it'd fit nice and snug in my inside pocket, but there was no way I could get it in there without being seen. With a bit of surreptitious fiddling about, I managed to slide part of it up my sleeve and hide the other end in my hand. With any luck, the Ugly Twins wouldn't decide to frisk us when we got out the car.

Reaching the end of the track, we pulled into what must at one time have been a farmyard, but had morphed into a rambling collection of dilapidated buildings and rusty machinery.

The car slithered to a halt and Benchy jumped out. Carol squeezed my hand. She was visibly shaking.

'It'll be fine, pet,' I said, keeping my voice low. Her monkey friend was already hauling her out the car.

I waited for Bench to open my door. With his mate still at the other side, I made like I was struggling to get out of the tight space and deliberately half fell onto the overgrown concrete. On my hands and knees, I was facing away from him and had just enough time to slip the spanner into my inside pocket. Whether I'd have a chance to use it was another matter entirely.

Gorilla Boy waved his gun and the four of us started towards the main building. Benchy produced a torch and moved in front of us, kicking open the door. It swung backwards, revealing some sort of workshop. There were shelves and workbenches along one wall, several rickety chairs, a table and a couple of gas cylinders, along with a few crates and what looked like an industrial space heater. Three wind-up lanterns lay on the table.

Mr Bench indicated the lamps and I correctly interpreted his grunts as a desire that I should get them working. Picking up the first one I unfastened the handle and started winding. It was an oddly satisfying experience to see the thing light up after a few seconds. I continued with this until instructed to do the same with the others.

Bench ordered Carol to sit down while I was otherwise employed. Furry Face attached the space heater to a couple of car batteries and a sudden whoosh of intense heat and noise filled the room. Continuing my winding activities, wondering why they were bothering to heat the place, I glanced up at Bench Face. His expression of total glee told me what he already knew - that the space heater was there for other reasons than keeping us warm.

With all the lamps lit, Monkey Boy arranged them in suitable locations. The overall effect was almost homely. However, our 'comfort' didn't last.

Bench made me sit me on a chair against the wall. The Bearded One kept the gun aimed at me while his pal tied Carol to hers.

When they were satisfied, Benchy pulled something out of the pocket of his overalls. It looked like a couple of sardines wrapped in brown paper. I guessed that's where the smell had come from.

'You making supper?' I said.

Bench laughed. 'Hear that? Supper, he says!' They both sniggered in a way that was not reassuring. 'No mate, just a little demonstration.'

Rooting around in a tea chest, he pulled out a long metal spike with three prongs on one end. I assumed it must be either an old-fashioned toasting fork or a particularly evil instrument of torture. Taking the sardines, he chucked one of them onto the table, skewered the other onto the tines and walked over to the space heater.

'Watch.' Moving the fork gradually closer to the glowing element, we watched as the skin began to sizzle, burn and finally, turn black. I was partial to a bit of grilled cod, but this guy's technique did nothing for my appetite.

Examining his handiwork, Bench strolled over to me. 'I'm sure a cocky twat like you can appreciate what that was in aid of, but just in case...' He swung the fork towards me, holding the singed mess in front of my face. 'That's what happens when a bit of flesh gets too close to the fire. So the plan is that you answer our questions, or we'll try the same thing...' He turned to Carol and pointed the fork at her.

'With the bonny lass, here. Okay?'

Carol's eyes went like saucers. She swallowed noisily.

'So,' Benchy continued, waving the fork around, 'Why don't ye tell us what ye know, eh?'

The Beard Monger was standing a few feet away from Carol, holding the gun. The table was still between us, so it wouldn't have done a lot of good to lay into his mate. I wondered how Don Corleone would deal with this sort of situation. Finally, I nodded my head.

'All right,' I said, 'tell me what you know, and I'll give you the nod if I know about it as well.' I gave him my best stupid grin, though my lower lip was trembling so much it was on the verge of doing a shimmy-shimmy shake.

'By Christ, ye're a funny fucker, you are.'

I'd expected him to lash out, to knock me over, maybe give me some chance to yank out my secret weapon, but instead he just nodded to his mate.

'No!' Carol's voice was sharp and loud, reverberating off the bare walls. Monkey Boy took no notice and dragged her chair towards the space heater. She kicked out at him, catching him in the shin, but he didn't stop til the chair was about six feet away. Straightaway, I saw the effect the apparatus had on Carol - with the business end of the heater angled upwards, the hot air blew her hair like she was standing on the edge of an erupting volcano. She shut her eyes and leaned back in an effort to escape the intense heat. If they pushed her any closer, she'd fry for sure.

I had to do something, but Hairy-Faced Gun-Boy was now further away from me than before. I glanced at Benchy who was busy laughing at Carol's plight, the fork still in his right hand. He was half turned away from me and any minute now, he'd resume his interrogation. My eyes flicked around the room, desperate for something, anything to leap to my aid. And then I saw it - one dead eye peeking over the edge of the table.

Reaching up, I grasped the thing in the palm of my hand and dropped my arm to my side, just as Bench Face turned his attention back to me.

'Right. I think we've made the point, so it's your turn now, gobshite.' He snarled, adding another layer of hideousness to his repellent features. 'Spill it.'

Beard Boy had pulled Carol's chair back and now they were both staring at me. Carol was looking hotter than she ever had, and not in a sexy way.

I took a breath and looked up. 'Well, I could tell ye, but ye'd end up havin a meal with Luca Brasi.'

Mr Bench laughed. Then stopped, confusion and disbelief fighting for supremacy on his ugly mug. 'Ye what?'

'Eatin with the fishes.'

Right on cue his jaw dropped and my left hand shot across and stuffed the sardine into his gaping mouth. He reeled backwards, dropping the fork and clawing at his offended orifice, spitting out cold fish. I grabbed the spanner from my inside pocket and whacked him in the bollocks before bringing it back up for a smart crack across the side of his head.

As he stumbled backwards, I could hear his ape-like pal motoring into action, but I'd already dropped to the floor and rolled under the table. Emerging on the other side, my right leg was nicely positioned to kick his legs from under him. But he was too quick and skipped away. Even so, he wasn't fast enough for Carol - she threw herself and the chair backwards, catching him a nice one in the guts.

As his arse hit the ground, the knuckles of his right hand smashed hard on the floor and he let go his grip on the gun. I grabbed it and jumped up.

'Get back!' I took hold of the back of Carol's chair, dragging her away from the heater. The gun was surprisingly heavy and I had to concentrate to keep it levelled at our former captors. With my free hand, I started undoing the ropes holding Carol to the chair.

Then I noticed Monkey Boy and Bench Face were just standing there, watching, rubbing their various wounded parts. As if this was merely a fly in their once-perfect ointment, they seemed in no hurry to make a move, but equally, oddly unaffected by what I thought of as my particularly successful take-over bid. After a moment, Bench took a step forward. Holding out a hand, he said, 'Give me the gun.'

'Like fuck. Now get back.' When he didn't move, I tried again. 'I said back!'

He shook his head. 'Ye winnae use it, man.'

'Will I not? Try it an see.' The ropes holding Carol's arms were loose now and she stooped forward pulling at those around her legs.

'Just give me the gun.'

Carol jumped up and got behind me, her hands gripping my jacket. 'Kill him, Terry.' Her voice was low, but I knew she meant it. I glanced at her.

Bench Face laughed, though now I detected a flicker of doubt in his eyes. 'He would, pet, but he's soft as shite. Got nae balls.' He took another step forward.

And that's when I pulled the trigger.

Chapter 11

Had I actually intended shooting someone, I might well have done a bit of serious damage, but my objective was only to scare the pair of them. Like all good westerns, I imagined a ricochet off the floor in the vicinity of my enemy's foot might communicate the necessary message - that I was not to be messed with. However, there was no ricochet, western or otherwise, and the bullet went into Bench Face's right boot, popping a neat hole into the space where his big toe had been.

Carol screamed at the same time as my victim, though his was more girly and screechy than hers could ever be. Ape Man, thankfully, did not scream, but a hand flew to his mouth in a distinctly camp gesture and the look on his face demonstrated this particular scenario had not been explained to him as a possible consequence of their actions.

'You told me it weren't real,' he wailed at Benchy.

By now, his associate was sitting on the floor clutching his injured foot. 'Course Ah did, ye fuckin ponce. Ye wouldn't have done it otherwise.' He rocked back and forth, moaning quietly.

There was a strange, acrid smell coming from the weapon and I remember thinking it wasn't a smell I wanted to get used to. I looked at Apey and waved the gun, taking care to keep my fingers well away from the trigger. 'Ye thought it was a toy?'

He nodded vigorously. 'I'm a friggin labourer, not a villain. Only came along to help out, an that.'

'Not a hired thug, then?' I said.

He waved a shaking finger at Benchy. 'I'm his next-door neighbour. He promised me two-hundred quid for a couple of hours work.'

'And what about him? What does he do when he's not toasting sardines?'

Beard Man glared at his pal. 'He's a plasterer.'

'A plasterer...' I couldn't believe it. We'd been abducted by a couple of amateurs.

Carol had stayed behind me but now she stepped forward. Approaching the bearded non-professional, she smacked him a nice one across the face. 'Ye fuckin shite. Coulda kill iz, ye stupid sod.' She slapped him again for good measure.

I pointed the gun at Benchy. 'Where's me keys?'

'In me pocket.' His whole face had started to tremble.

I told him to throw them over to me. He made a big show of being in pain and not being able to function properly, but eventually the keys landed at my feet. Carol picked them up.

'Right,' I said. 'You,' indicating Beard Boy. 'Out you go.' I pointed at the door.

His eyes flicked between me and the exit. 'What, y'mean leave?'

'Yes.'

'But I don't know where we are.'

I shrugged. 'Not my problem.'

'How'm I meant to get home?'

'Again, not my problem.' I smiled at him and waggled my fingers. 'Off you go.'

With a final glare at Bench Face, he crossed to the door and went out. I waited a moment then told Carol to check he'd gone.

She peered out the door. 'Aye, runnin like his arse is on fire.'

I sat on the edge of the table. 'So, like I was saying before, you tell iz what ye know and I'll give you the nod if I know about it as well.'

Of course, it wasn't as easy as in the movies, where the bad guy coughs for all his misdeeds. Our foot-mangled friend was unable to furnish us with much more information than we already knew. It seemed he'd got involved through a small-time villain called Spanx, who'd offered him the job for a 'handling' fee. Bench Face swore he'd taken the work believing it'd boost his profile in the community and that the identity of the Mr or Mrs Big behind it all, was a mystery he hadn't been privy to.

As to why they were at the marina, it turned out that the 'brief' had included the location of the farm, outlined a few possible scenarios, and basically left the time and date to their own discretion. It just so happened the pair of pricks had followed us from the Hexagon on the off-chance it might lead to a Spanish Inquisition-type opportunity.

Even so, that particular scenario posed more questions than answers. Apart from us, only two other people knew what I was up to. There was Charis as well, of course, who at least knew I'd tailed the Swedish hunk from the restaurant, but I couldn't see her being part of some bent cop scheme. The only explanation had to be that one of my taxi-driver pals was auditioning for the part of Tesio, and making a damn good job of it.

I'd quite like to have shot Bench Face again, just to make a point, but I didn't think he had any reason to sell us another load of porkies, and as I hadn't intended shooting him in the first place, it would have been difficult to justify inflicting yet more pain and suffering on a dumb animal.

After taking a few pics of his driving licence and bank cards (just in case), we dropped him at the hospital on Rake's Lane, promising a follow-up visit if he was stupid enough to mention our names to anyone. As he clambered out, I leaned over the back of the seat.

'What about your car?'

His mouth dropped open. 'Aw, shit - I forgot.' He closed his eyes and for a moment I thought he might cry. 'It's me dad's. He'll fuckin kill iz.'

'Oh, well,' I said. 'Worse things happen at Quays.'

He frowned. 'What?'

'It's a joke. Worse things happen... Nah, forget it.'

As we pulled away from the main entrance, he gave me a wave, as if the whole thing had been some kind of jolly jape.

'I didn't mean it, ye know,' said Carol, examining her face in the drop-down mirror.

'Didn't mean what?' I pulled up at the exit and made a left.

'That ye should shoot.'

'Aye, that's what I thought.' I patted her leg.

She was quiet for a moment, then, 'We're not goin back to the marina, are we?'

'Think we've had enough excitement for one night. How does a hot bath and a soft bed sound?'

'Now hey - I'm definitely not goin to your sister's again.'

'No, I was thinking of summat a bit more rural. There's a nice little B and B just outside Morpeth. Should be far enough away to keep us out of trouble.'

She nodded and closed her eyes.

A metallic clanging woke me. At first, I couldn't imagine why there'd be a steel band in a guesthouse, then I remembered the small pair of gongs we'd noticed in the hallway on our arrival. Mrs Henderson had said she'd give us a bang in the morning. I'd assumed she was being cheeky.

My room was at the back of the house and looked towards the Cheviot hills. If it hadn't been for the rain and the fog, I might have been able to see them. Sharon and me had stopped off there one weekend for reasons that escaped me, but the place hadn't changed much - it was warm and comfortable and for the first time in ages, I actually felt rested.

The en suite shower was a blast in more ways than one, and by the time I emerged, it felt like I'd washed a week's worth of dirt and tension away.

According to my mobile, it was just after eight o'clock. There were a few texts (Lizzy, Fat Barry, Ronnie), and a voicemail from our favourite Detective Inspector. There was also a text on the Carver mobile, but I decided to ignore it for now. I got dressed and knocked on Carol's door. She peeked out and said she'd be a couple of minutes. I was halfway down the stairs before it hit me.

Ronnie?

Clicking on the message, I stared at it:

Give it back!

Oh, Christ.

Had the police confiscated Ronnie's phone? I cast my mind back to that day at Charis's place when we'd gone through everything. There'd been no mention of a mobile, but that didn't mean they didn't have it, and surely if they hadn't found it, Charis would've mentioned it. I listened to her voicemail - she wanted to know if I knew anything about a young guy who'd turned up at North Tyneside General with his toe blown off. Presumably, Bench Face had kept schtum, but I had to wonder why Charis assumed I was involved.

When Carol appeared at the breakfast table, I'd already had three cups of coffee and a bowl of porridge.

'What's the plan, Batman?' She was looking better than a smack in the face and her smile told me she was happier than she'd been for days.

'Couple of things to check.' I passed her the photo of Andersson from the News Post and pointed to the round-faced councillor standing next to the Swede. 'Wanna pay him a visit. See if he remembers anything about Frank. But first we're going to have a little drink in the North Sea.'

Bench Face had told us where we might find the low-life known as Spanx, though he'd begged me not to mention where we'd got the information. I smiled sweetly and promised I'd drop him in the shit at the first opportunity.

The rain let off a bit as we headed back to the coast and by the time we reached our destination, it was almost a nice day. I took a slow run past the pub, in case there were any obvious lurkers, but it seemed quiet enough.

Nipping into a private car park at the back of Dilys McKinley's Liquor Emporium, I reversed behind a wall out of sight of the road. The place had closed down a few months before after a drugs raid, so there was no fear of wheel clamps and the like.

We skipped across the street and down the side entrance into the North Sea. The smell emanating from the toilets was as bad as ever but I didn't mind breathing it in for a few seconds while I took a peek through into the Snug Bar. The customary pre-lunch crowd of no-hopers and wasters were at their regular tables, but I doubted any of them had the nous to shoulder the mantle of small-time villainy.

Carol clutched my hand. 'We goin ter stand here

all day?'

I moved along to the door of the lounge bar and walked in. It was another case of the usual suspects, though there were a few faces I didn't recognise.

'Alreet Terry? Heard ye were back on the cabs.' Brian was polishing glasses with a general lack of enthusiasm. He finished what he was doing and leaned on the bar. Winking at Carol, he muttered, 'Not seen you in here for a while, bonny lass? Shaggin him now, are ye?'

'For God's sake,' she said. 'Why does everybody think we're at it? Can't a couple of friends go into a pub just for the company?'

Brian humphed and glared round at the assembled drinkers. 'Nobody comes in here for the company.' He looked at me. 'What ye after?'

I moved forward and dropped my voice. 'Ye know a bloke called Spanx?'

He shook his head. 'No, but I know a *woman* called Spanx.' He deliberately moved his eyes to the right.

I followed his gaze towards the end of the bar. A dark-haired woman was sitting on a barstool at the corner, drinking from a tall glass that had a table-decoration balanced on top. She was wearing a frilly blouse, short black skirt, six-inch heels and a pair of fishnet stockings. From here, she looked like a good time on a Friday night, but I knew her best years were a long way behind her.

'Her?'

Brian nodded. 'Apparently Spanx is her new

business name.'

Carol gave me a knowing look. 'Ye can do that bit of business on your own.' She tapped on the bar. 'Half a lager please, Bri.'

'Get me one as well,' I said, taking a deep breath.

Judy was concentrating on playing some irritating kids game on her mobile. She looked up as I approached. 'Ooh, hello Terry. Fancy seein you here.' Reaching out a hand, she stroked my arm. Her wrists were thicker than mine and her tattoos would put a seasoned sailor to shame.

I forced a smile, trying to ignore the deep furrows that ran in criss-cross patterns over her face. I knew she must be over fifty, but close-up she'd easily pass for eighty-three.

'Can I get ye a drink?'

She giggled, showing off her light brown teeth. 'Of course ye can, Terry, but what're ye after, eh?' She licked her lips in a way that didn't send chills or anything else down my spine.

Waving a hand at Brian, I indicated another glass of whatever brand of piss she was drinking. 'Just needin a bit of information, pet.'

She narrowed her eyes and I could almost hear the cogs going round. Leaning an elbow on the bar, she switched off her phone and let out a long sigh.

'Everything costs money, these days.'

I waited, thinking she might expand on this, but she didn't so I pressed on. 'Ye were talking to a friend of mine the other day. Peter Haddock.'

Her face creased up, adding another ten years to

her age. 'Oh, aye - Peter. The lad wi' the face like a welded bench. Aye, canny lad.'

'Ye gave him some money for a job. I was just wondering who you were...representin.'

Her mouth opened and her head dropped to one side. She looked at me for a long moment while the coinage dropped into place. Eventually, her eyes widened. 'Oh, fuck.'

I nodded encouragingly. 'Go on...'

'Look, Terry, I was telt you'd had yer hand in the till, been rippin somebody off and they had to teach ye a lesson.' She pawed my chest as if physical contact might support her claim to innocence.

'Details would be good.'

She shuffled round and tugged at her skirt.

'All I had to do was give him an envelope. Money and instructions, ye know - like on Mission Impossible. Ye have tae believe me, Terry, I didn't know what they were up to.'

'Ye knew it was me they were after, though?'

She shook her head so hard, I felt the draft. 'No, I really didn't, man.'

'Where did the job come from? And come to think of it, why did they give it to you?'

Brian sauntered up and placed another garish drink in front of her.

She waited until he'd gone back to the other end of the bar. 'Cos I know folk.'

This was true. In fact, Judy's intimate knowledge of the less-salubrious members of the town's male population might well furnish her with a regular income in the blackmail stakes. 'Who gave you the job?'

She shook her head. 'Cannit tell ye that, bonny lad. He's me best client.' She paused. 'Well, not him, but he gets me a lot of business, if ye know what I mean?'

I did. 'I just need his name, Judy.'

Her mouth turned down in a sad-clown sort of way and she shrugged helplessly. 'Sorry.'

I nodded as if I'd expected this. 'Fine. When I see Mr Ahmed I'll tell him you were a big help.' I started to turn away, but she grabbed my arm.

'What ye say?'

'Ahmed.'

She sniggered. 'Nah.' She wiggled a finger at me in a 'naughty-boy' motion. 'Nice try, Terry.'

'But ye do know him?'

'Aye, but only by reputation.'

That wasn't what I wanted to hear. But I still had another option. 'So it was Andersson you dealt with?'

Her face was blank. Not a flicker. 'Never heard of him.'

'Right. Thanks for your help, Judy.'

'Anytime, luvver.'

I rejoined Carol and gave her the gist of the conversation.

'So we're no further forward?'

Taking a sip of my lager, I pulled out my wallet. Handing Brian a twenty, I slid the newspaper cutting across the bar. 'Any idea where this feller hangs out, Bri?'

He sniffed and raised the paper to his face, squinting at the image. 'Donny White. Town councillor and lover of large breasts.' He dropped his voice. 'Has a bit of a fancy for young blokes as well, apparently.' He passed the photo back. 'Hangs out at the Con club, or ye'll get him at his work.'

'And where might that be?'

Chapter 12

They built the West Links Community Centre in the mid-Seventies, when the idea of working with local people in ways that might enable them to contribute towards their own communities was all the rage. Since then the place had gone downhill and the role of the person in charge was less about engaging folk in worthwhile activities and more to do with keeping them occupied on wet afternoons.

We stood in the entrance hall listening to the monotonous tones of the bingo caller. A face appeared in the hatch to our left.

'Can Ah help ye, pet?'

Waving my council tax form in front of her, I slipped it back into my jacket before she'd a chance to put on her spectacles. 'Could we see Mr White? We're here about the lease.'

She cocked a hand around one ear. 'Ye what, pet?'

'The lease.'

The old woman's eyes opened wide. 'Oh, well, aye, he's doin the bingo just now.' She patted at her hair. 'Be finished by dinnertime, if ye's want to wait?' She smiled at Carol. 'Ye's want a cup of tea or anything?'

'No thanks.'

She disappeared again and we wandered over to the double doors at the end of the hallway. Through the two squares of fireproof glass, we could see the recreation room and a group of around forty older folks sitting at rows of trestle tables, heads bent in concentration. Beyond them, a lone figure sat at a smaller table, hunched over an electronic bingo machine.

'All the fours, forty-four.' Pause. 'One and six, sixteen.' Pause. 'Three and five –'

'Hoose!' An arm shot up out of the crowd, waving a pink sheet. 'Here ye are.'

A young woman, who must have been standing off at one side, gravitated towards the winner and proceeded to check the numbers on the sheet.

'I could never understand the attraction of that game,' said Carol. 'I'd rather watch football, and that's sayin summat.'

The wall beside the doors was plastered with photographs and the occasional headline pertaining to the success of the centre's activities. Peering at the images, I was able to pick out Donny White, his grinning face always nearest the lens, clearly demonstrating his interpersonal skills: Donny with the youth club, Donny dishing out Christmas Lunch, Donny filling in funding applications, Donny and his pals from the Conservative Club holding up one of those giant cheques. He certainly had the knack of smiling for the camera, which made me wonder why that particular facial expression was lacking in our photo.

Ten minutes later, the winners and losers spilled out of their enclosure and amid much waving and chattering began to exit the building.

The young woman who'd checked the bingo cards, followed behind and said hello as she passed, then added 'Ye's after Donny? He'll be out in a minute.' Pulling a pack of cigarettes from her back pocket, she lit up before reaching the door, generously sharing her out-breath. The smoke hung in the hallway like a small cloud.

We waited a moment then the man himself trundled through the double doors, head down, making a beeline for the office where our friendly tea-maker lived.

Though I couldn't see their faces, I caught snatches of an irritated exchange that gave way to more placatory expressions. After a bit of thumping around that sounded remarkably like a temper tantrum, our host appeared at the office door.

'Ah, hello, ahm..?' He was a small hairless bloke with a fat belly. In real life, he didn't quite match the image of the busy working community worker depicted on the notice board and I wondered how many years had passed since he'd last done any proper work.

'Davidson.' I grasped the proffered hand and shook it for the appropriate amount of time. His grip felt artificially firm and I already knew I wasn't going to like this man.

His face stretched into a smile and he looked at Carol.

'And this is..?'

Carol glanced at me, then said, 'Harley.'

The fat man nodded. His eyes flitted between my face and Carol's chest until I coughed and asked if there was somewhere we could talk.

'Here's fine,' he said, with only a smidgen of irritation.

In a voice loud enough for Tea Woman to hear, I said, 'We'd like a word about Sven Andersson.'

Donny quickly shunted his colleague out of the office and made a big show of placing a wooden board across the hatch. He wasted a few minutes gathering files and papers from his desk and sliding them onto a shelf by the window. Eventually he sat down opposite us.

'Now, how can I help? I've got a Council meeting at two so I can't be long.' He was breathing heavily, but I wasn't sure if it was a result of his frantic bingo activities or the mention of his favourite builder.

Sliding the photo across the desk, I watched his face carefully. Oddly, he didn't pick it up. Instead, he bent his head forward to study the image. After what seemed like an inordinately long time, he looked up.

'Yes, I remember. New development. Houses for the disenfranchised, sort of thing.'

'How well d'you know Mr Andersson?'

He shrugged exaggeratedly. 'Hardly at all, actually.'

'So you didn't have dinner with him recently?' This was a wild guess but he almost jumped off his chair.

'Dinner? Oh, well, yes. Once or twice, maybe.'

'And did you discuss Frank Armstrong and Ronnie Thompson?'

'Now here, I never had nowt to do with that and, as it happens, neither did Mr Andersson.'

'I didn't say you had anything to do with anything, Mr White.'

'Didn't ye? Oh. Right.' He licked his lips and stumbled on. 'I mean, ye know, I read about it, the mur...the murder, an that. In the paper. Never met either of them, though. The er...dead...erm...people.'

Leaning forward, I rested my elbows on the desk, closing the space between us. 'Really? But Frank Armstrong was there when this photo was taken.'

He swallowed and looked again at the picture. 'But he's not...' He looked up, panic etched across his face. 'He's not...'

'Not in the photo? No.'

He glanced at Carol. 'But...'

My sidekick jumped in. 'How d'ye know he's not in the photo if you don't know what he looked like?'

'I...I just assumed.'

'Why was Frank there that day?' I leaned back and waited.

'Well, cos he...' He let out a long, weary sigh. 'Because he picked us up. From the Hexagon.'

'Ye'd had lunch together? You an Andersson?'

He nodded.

'So why did Frank hang around?'

'We'd been drinkin, hadn't we? Frank - Mr Armstrong - dropped me at home after.'

'And what about Andersson? Where'd he go

afterwards?'

He shook his head. 'I couldn't say.'

Carol tapped my leg and mouthed 'Ahmed'. I nodded. 'And how well d'you know Mr Ahmed?'

For the second time, our fat friend visibly started. 'Ahmed? Not at all, not at all. Never met him.'

'Sure about that? Never been to his house on Nugent Crescent? You know, where they have the girls?'

His head swung from side to side, like a ball boy at Wimbledon. After a long pause, he said, 'I was never invited.' At that, his eyes closed and he clasped his hands together as if he were about to say a prayer.

'Anything else ye want to tell us?'

'No.' He rubbed his face, fat jowls wobbling like a fleshy jelly. Then, dropping his head, said, 'Will I have to make a statement?'

Carol sniggered, and I coughed loudly to cover it. 'Why would ye have to make a statement, Mr White?'

He looked at Carol, then at me. 'For your records?'

'We're not the police.'

He sat up straight. 'You're not?' His head jerked to the hatch. 'Mavis said ye's were from the police.'

Biting my lip to keep from laughing, I said, 'Mavis a bit deaf, is she?'

His mouth opened and closed. 'Well who the hell are ye, then?' His voice had risen considerably in tone and there was now more than a hint of hostility.

I guessed it was time to go. 'Just a couple of interested parties, Donny. Cheers for your time.'

As I made for the door, the little man stamped his feet. 'Now just hold on a fuckin minute...' But we were already in the hall and heading for safety.

'That was interesting,' said Carol as we pulled back into traffic.

'But again, we didn't learn much. This whole Andersson stroke Ahmed thing could just be about a group of blokes in each other's pockets. Backhanders and the like.'

'An women on the side as well?' Carol shook her head. 'Not exactly above board though, is it?'

'No, but it doesn't mean they've killed anyone.'

She turned and stared at me. 'Maybe not, but somebody's killing people and in case ye'd forgotten, they've had a couple of goes at killing us.'

She was right, but even so, it felt like we were constantly running into dead-ends. My head was stuffed with things that didn't make sense, and I didn't have a clue what to do next. When I said as much to Carol, she laughed.

'It's obvious.'

'Is it?'

'Aye. We know when the photo was taken, and we know Frank was definitely there, so we have to get back to the office and check the job sheets from that day.'

'Right.' I frowned. 'Why?'

She gave me one of her for-fuck's-sake sighs. 'So we can see where he went after they took the photo, of course.'

'Donny said Frank took him home.'

'An ye believe him?'

I parked at Dilys McKinley's place again and we pulled on a couple of woolly hats in a bid to hide our faces. Keeping to the back streets, we got to the taxi office just after one o'clock. I'd replied to Fat Barry's text earlier to tell him we wouldn't be in, so I wasn't sure what sort of reception we'd get turning up out of the blue.

The girl on the desk was a stranger and there was no sign of Ken or any of the other drivers.

'Hi there,' she said cheerily, swinging round in her chair. 'Ye's wantin a taxi?'

'Who are you?' Carol glared at her and slid behind the counter to look at the old job sheets.

The young woman glanced at me. 'I'm Chrissy. Just started.'

'Jumping into me bloody grave, more like.' Carol rifled through the papers and passed a bundle to me.

'Ken's not in, is he?' I adopted a neutral tone, in an effort to combat Carol's irritation.

'Erm...' She fidgeted with the tassels on her cardigan as she watched Carol trash the place. 'He's gone home. Wasn't feeling well.' She looked up at me. 'His son died, ye know?' She made a mournful face, in case we didn't understand.

'Aye, I know.' I wandered over to Ken's office but it was locked.

A voice crackled over the radio. 'Hey pet, d'ye knaa where this Robson bloke lives? I canna find the hoose.'

Chrissy picked up the current job sheet and peered at it. 'She clicked the mic. 'The man just said it was Hopton Heath lane off Hopton Heath Road. So...' She bit her lip.

'C'mere.' Carol grabbed the mic. 'That you, Jimmy? It's a regular customer. The flat's not actually on Hopton Heath Lane - it's round the back on the corner of Naseby Road. Ye'll see a metal staircase going up to it.'

The voice crackled back, 'Cheers Carol, ye're a star. Hey, ye back at work?'

Carol gave the mic back to Chrissy. 'No, I'm bloody not.' She held up a bundle of papers. 'Cops must've brought back the sheets for Friday and Saturday. Worth a look, eh?'

I nodded. 'Maybe.'

In the car, we split the pile into two and started going through them. I had the ones for the days leading up to when the photograph had been taken, so ran through the pickups Frank had done. I couldn't see anything unusual about any of them - just the same old rank-to-Tesco's, Tesco-to-North-Shields, Shields-to-town, rank-to-Landsdowne, rank-to-Inkerman and so on.

On the day of the photo, Frank had cleared in town and picked up from the Hexagon at 1:35 pm.

He'd called clear at Marston Road ten minutes later. Marston Road was right next to the building site where Andersson's new development was situated. Frank hadn't called in his next pickup until half an hour later, when he did Marston-to-Tudor-Grange. I wondered if Councillor Donny lived near my sister.

'Hey,' Carol said. 'Look at this.' She pointed to a job Frank had called in on the night he died. 'Picked up a flag-down from town to the Bull's Head. And then, guess what? Bull's-Head-to-Otterburn.' She blinked several times. 'That's where you live, Terry.'

'Aye.' I made a 'so-what' gesture.

'Didn't see Frank that night, did ye?'

'Well...'

'Cos ye told the fuzz ye were fixin your car and we both know that's a fuckin lie, don't we? You know less about cars than I do and that isn't a bloody lot.' Her mouth was tight and she was breathing quicker than usual, as if she was a little bit pissed off. 'Somethin ye want to tell me, Terry?'

Rubbing a hand over my face, I took my time answering. It was bound to come out sooner or later. I'd been hoping for the second option, but it seemed that stringing out the truth, like our investigation, had hit a dead end.

'Yes, I saw him.' Keeping my eyes on the sheaf of papers in my lap, I waited for the lecture. But it didn't come. I could hear her breathing, slower now and measured. Out the corner of my eye, I caught the shake of the head, the for-fuck's-sake expression.

Eventually, she spoke. 'Goin to tell me, then?'

I moved my head slightly towards her. 'He dropped a punter at the Bull and I was in there having a pint, so I got him to run me home.'

Carol shrugged. 'And?'

'When we got to mine, we just sat in the car an talked.' I hesitated. 'Frank was plannin to leave Lizzy.' I took a breath. 'You know what she's like - always treated him like shit, talked about him behind his back, shagged his mates. All he wanted was for her to be happy, but in the end, she wasn't interested in him. I think he finally realised he was just a meal ticket. Anyway, he met someone else - by chance, ye know. A young Syrian woman.'

'Oh, God, you're jokin?' She turned to face me. 'Illegal immigrant? Lap dancer? Of course, and Frank being a man past his prime, it wouldn't be hard to turn his head. Tch, typical.'

'It wasn't like that, Carol. He cared about her.'

'Oh, you know her, do ye?'

'No, but –'

'But nothing. I bet ye'd have fancied her an'all.'

'Told ye, I didn't meet her.' I paused for a moment, remembering the conversation I'd had with Frank that night - sitting in his car drinking, with him pouring out his heart and me telling him to stop being so bloody stupid, that she was probably living here illegally and would fleece him for every penny he had. I'd sounded a lot like Carol.

'I thought I'd persuaded him to leave her alone, that he'd end up getting hurt. But he just got angry, said I was hardly in a position to dish out advice what with my girlfriend upstairs packing her bags. He kicked me out the car and drove off.'

Carol picked at her fingernails. 'So what then? Where did he go after that?'

I leaned over and looked at the job sheet. 'He called in a couple of fake jobs while he was with me so you'd think he was still driving. He gave me the impression he was plannin to see his lady friend to sort things out.' I ran my finger down the job list. 'That must've been about nine.'

'So why did ye not tell the cops? What difference would it have made?'

'Seeing him laid out on the table, I thought he must have changed his mind, maybe told her it was over. So it didn't seem fair to tell Lizzy. Specially when I didn't know for sure.'

Carol nodded. 'Aye, I suppose.'

I cleared my throat. 'There's something else.'

'What?' She prodded my leg. '*What*, Terry?'

'When I went back upstairs, Sharon was still sorting stuff out. I didn't want to get in the way, so I went for another couple of beers then walked around for a bit. Eventually, I went down to Frank's place. Thought maybe I could smooth things over, talk him round.'

'And?'

'The front door was open, ye know - on the latch. Frank was there, on the table.' I closed my eyes for a moment. 'He was dead.'

'What time was that?'

'Late. About half twelve, one, maybe.'

Carol leaned over and grabbed the job sheets. 'So what did he do after he left you?' She peered at the list of jobs. 'I gave him a couple of contracts on the Andersson account.' She tapped the sheet. 'There, two pickups from two different office complexes - that was six o'clock, then another one just after ten from the industrial estate down to...' She looked up. 'The Hexagon.' She passed the sheets back. 'Then he signed off.'

We sat in silence for a while, until Carol said, 'You think this foreign woman might be involved with Ahmed's lot? Like a sex-slave or summat?'

'It had occurred to me. Though the first night when I dropped Elise off, it just looked like any other party.'

'Aye but didn't ye say a couple of the guys almost had their shirts off?'

'They did, but that doesn't mean anything. Elise was still dressed and the people I could see in the other windows all had their clothes on. In any case, they weren't trying to hide anything, which ye'd expect if there was something dodgy going on. They'd at least close the curtains.'

Carol swivelled round in her seat. 'So, if Frank had dropped Elise off at that house before and maybe, I don't know, maybe seen his girlfriend in there as well..?'

'Hang on.' I went back to the sheets I'd been looking through. If Frank had made several drop-offs to the house, maybe he already knew there was something going on. 'Here, the week before, he dropped Elise at Central Station.' I looked up. 'That's where she was supposed to be goin when I dropped her off, so this one could easily have ended up being a Nugent Crescent job.' I checked the next night and there it was again, though this time the pickup had been from one of the offices. 'Maybe a few of Andersson's employees or associates were meeting up at the house? I mean, if it was just folks getting together for a drink or summat after work, why would they traipse all the way to Newcastle?'

She nodded. 'Why indeed. So what now?'

'Now? I reckon we should crash a party.'

Chapter 13

In the lane behind Nugent Crescent, it was darker than on my previous visit.

'Can't see a bloody thing here ye know,' said Carol, clutching my hand.

'Ye'll be able to in a minute.' We followed the wall down to the gate where I'd been so rudely interrupted before. Warning Carol to keep a lookout for Cockney Jamaicans, I put a foot onto the baton and hoisted myself up. Unlike before, there was nothing to see. Though the curtains were open, all the rooms in the house were in darkness. There were no signs of life.

As I jumped down, I fell against the gate. There was a click and somewhat bizarrely, it swung open. I glanced at Carol, but it was too dark to see her expression. 'Open sez me.'

'Ye're not going in?'

'Why not, place is empty.' I pushed the gate and peered into the yard. The two motorcycles were still chained up to the wall and the table and chairs were still on the patio.

Carol tugged at my sleeve. 'Terry!'

'What?'

'I don't know - just don't do anything stupid.'

'As if.' Crossing to the back door, I cupped my hands against the glass. It was pitch black inside. I beckoned to my accomplice. 'Where's the torch?'

She fished in her jacket pocket and pulled out a Maglite with a length of string attached to the end. I popped the loop around my neck in case I dropped it, then holding the torch close to the glass, switched it on. There still wasn't much to see - the door led to a passage and into the kitchen. The entrance to the latter was half open, revealing a long table and a few chairs, but little else. I moved across to the next window - what I presumed to be the living room. There were a couple of long sofas and several armchairs, along with a small coffee table. Against one wall were bookcases filled with DVDs, though what their subject matter might be, I couldn't tell.

And then the light came on.

I jumped back and Carol let out a squeak. The light from the living room lit up the yard and must have leaked into the room next door as well, for the previously darkened kitchen was now partially lit. We stood pressed flat up against the narrow wall between the back door and the window. If we moved, whoever was inside might see us.

'This is another fine mess,' whispered Carol.

I leaned over to her. 'We'll be all right so long as they don't come outside.'

Which, of course, is when someone decided to come outside.

I heard the footsteps advancing along the passage. Then the fiddling with the lock and the rattle of the handle. I was about to scream 'run' and drag Carol out into the lane, when the noise stopped. Maybe they'd changed their minds?

Perhaps just checking the place was secure? Yes, that must be it.

And then the door opened.

The giant of a man who stepped into the yard clearly hadn't expected to encounter visitors, for his shout was almost as loud as mine.

'Jesusfuckinhell!' He aimed a fist in my direction, but only succeeded in hitting my shoulder. I grabbed his arm and gave it a yank.

'Terry? What the fuck?'

I let go his arm. 'Ralph? What you doin here?'

'Keep your voice doon, man.' He glanced around, then ushered us both inside.

'Well, bonny lad,' said Ralph helping himself to a beer from the fridge, 'if ye'd answer the bloody phone, we'd know what ye were up to, wouldn't we?'

'Sorry. I meant to call back.'

'Aye, aye, whatever. So, as I was saying, Mrs Carver's not the type to wait around for answers and since you were dragging your proverbials, she sent me to check this place out.'

I frowned. 'How d'you know where it was?'

'Unlike you, when I dae a bit of surveillance work, I dae it properly. See, when you pair of daft twats turned up here the other night with the fancy masks on, I was over the road watching.'

'Over the road?'

He jerked a thumb towards the front of the house. 'My sister's lad has the upstairs flat. When I saw your car come down here, I parked up the top and ran along the back way. An by the way, I have to tell ye, mate, ye're not hard to follow - I could have stayed five cars behind and ye'd still have stuck oot like a sore dick.' He chuckled and took another swig of lager.

Carol butted in. 'You followed us? Ye cheeky sod.'

'Oh aye.' I nodded. 'The Volvo with the tinted windows?'

'That's the one. Great for keepin an eye of folk when ye divvent want to get noticed.'

'We did notice the car, actually,' said Carol. 'We're not totally stupid.'

He grinned. 'Anyhow, the next day, I got the lad to take over for a while, so he's been watchin the place since then.'

'And?'

He scowled. 'Seems there's a lot of individuals in and out, but without having a look inside, we'd no idea if they just like to party of if there's summat else gannin on. So when the lad called iz to say Ahmed and his cronies had all piled into their cars and taken off, I thought I'd have a look.'

'When did they leave?' I asked, suddenly concerned they might return.

'Charlie says they took a load of bags an that, so I reckon they're away for the night at least.'

I had to admit the furnishings were tasteful. Upstairs, there were three large bedrooms and a bathroom with a walk-in shower. Each bedroom was done out in pastel shades with matching furniture. Checking through the wardrobes, there was nothing untoward, and apart from the lack of mess, the place could have been the home of an average suburban family with teenage kids.

The only moment of excitement was a cash box Ralph found wedged under one of the beds. Producing a set of skeleton keys, he got it open in a couple of minutes, but there were no illicit diamonds or bags of crystal meth, only two passports in the name of Sanjay and Gita Ahmed. All apparently above board.

Back downstairs, we gathered in the kitchen.

'You disappointed?' said Ralph.

'Well, I'm kinda glad we didn't find half a dozen eastern European women tied to the beds with chains an that, but yes, I'm disappointed.'

Leaning against the kitchen table, it felt as if yet another lead had led us into a cul-de-sac. If Mr Ahmed was up to something, he was doing a great job of hiding the evidence.

Carol grabbed my arm. 'What's that?' Her head jerked towards the front of the house. We turned towards the sound. Then a buzzing came from Ralph's jacket.

Pulling out his phone, he listened, muttered, 'Aye, we kinda realised that,' and put it away. 'Ahmed's back.'

We were through the kitchen door in a second, ignoring the fact we'd left all the lights on. The gate to the lane was still open and if we'd been a bit quicker we might have made it. Unfortunately, the man called Horse was now blocking our exit route.

'Who the fuck are you?'

There was no possibility of getting past him that I could see, but Ralph clearly thought it was worth a go. Rushing past me, he aimed his head at Horse's stomach and barged into him. Somehow, the big feller managed to avoid injury and Ralph ended up flat on his face with Horse standing over him.

Carol slipped her fingers into mine and I glanced back towards the kitchen, but there were already two men in the open doorway. I looked at Ralph and my stomach did a quick flip when I saw he wasn't moving. The giant who'd floored him stepped into the yard.

'I'll ask ye's again - who the fuck *are* ye?'

Whatever I was about to say must remain a mystery. The fist that slammed into my face knocked me backwards. I fell over Carol, hit the floor and everything went black.

The bed was not the one I'd expected to wake up in. In fact, it wasn't a bed at all. I blinked several times, trying to focus on my surroundings, but it was too dark to see very much. Moving my fingers across my body, it was a relief to find I was still dressed. It was slightly less of a relief to find something sticky under my nose. As soon as I touched it, the pain surged up my face. I had a vague memory of being in the back of a van, of my head being used to wipe the floor.

Struggling to sit up, I closed my eyes, the dull ache across my forehead coming in waves. After a minute, it began to diminish and I was able to open my eyes again. Looking around, the darkness lay heavily over everything. Spreading my hands out, I began to feel my way around the space, exploring the area where I'd lain, then moving across the room.

I'd been lying on a piece of rough fabric - canvas or sacking maybe. Underneath, a cold draught wafted up through the floorboards. I smoothed the material back down and my fingers came into contact with an object next to me - something big, something warm.

'Ralphy? That you?' My voice sounded hoarse and I coughed a few times to dislodge whatever was holding back my usual dulcet tones. 'Ralphy?'

The bundle groaned and struggled into a sitting position. 'Divvent call iz Ralphy, ye dick.'

'Sorry.'

My eyes were getting used to the darkness and now I could see a dim outline - two rectangular-shaped panels on opposite walls. Struggling to my knees, I crawled across the floor and felt around the edges of the nearest one. If this was a window here, it'd been expertly boarded up. The slither of pale light illuminating the edges, might've been cast by a dull sun on a rainy day, or a pale moon on a black night.

It was only then that I remembered Carol. Why

hadn't they brought her here as well? Surely it'd be easier to keep us all in one place? I thought the truth was probably less complicated - I knew why they'd split us up and it wasn't an image I wanted in my head. Whatever they were up to, it reeked of something much worse than simply being locked away.

Crawling around the edge of the room, I discovered that apart from the two boarded-up windows, there was only one door (locked, of course), and an overall space no bigger than twelve feet square. Its only occupants were me and my big mate.

Ralph was sitting up rubbing his head. 'Where's the lassie?'

'Not here.'

'Shite.'

Ralph stood up and started patting his pockets. 'Your phone gone?'

I checked and nodded, then remembered he couldn't see me. 'Yeah, both of them.' I went through my clothes and found they'd taken my wallet too, leaving only a few coins, a hanky and...something hard sticking in my armpit. Pulling my shirt open, I slipped a hand inside and found the torch. It must have dropped in there when I hit the deck.

Pulling the string over my head, I switched the Maglite on. Ralph swore and held a hand up, wincing.

'Where'd that come from?'

'It's Carol's. Forgot to give it back.' Now we had light, we searched the room properly. Sadly, there was nothing else significant or useful, but it was obvious from the decor that we weren't in a house. The walls seemed to be built from smooth concrete blocks and were doing a good impression of being solidly constructed. Apart from a few scuff marks, the floorboards were clean. 'Some sort of industrial unit?'

Ralph nodded. 'Two storey at least. And new.' Dropping to his knees, he pulled back the canvas I'd been sitting on and sniffed the wood. 'Aye. See?' He pointed to small holes in the planks. 'Ye can still see the tops of the nails. Shiny, see? Haven't had time to get dirty.' He crawled along the floor while I shone the torch over his shoulder. 'Bloody amateurs, haven't even used tongue and groove. Wankers.' Pushing down on the floor, he continued along, testing the boards. Finally, he stood up. 'What they used to call jerry built.'

I waved the torch over the floorboards. 'Looks fine to me.'

'Wood hasn't been seasoned, ye can see where it's already startin to come up. An there...' He tapped a foot. 'They've only nailed every third or fourth plank.'

'Aye, well when we get out I'll report them to building standards.'

He gave me a playful smack across the back of the head. 'Ye daftie - this is our way out.'

I looked at the floor. 'It is?'

Ralph took the Maglite and scanned the room. 'Just need summat to give us a bit of leverage...'

I watched him walking around the room, covering every inch of the space with the light. It was reassuring that he was keen to escape, but I couldn't imagine how that was going to happen.

'Here we go.' Ralph was staring at the ceiling.

'Plasterboard?'

He nodded, grinning. 'Not just plasterboard, shoddy workmanship.'

'I'm not with you.'

He chewed his lip, humming some random tune. Then grasping my shoulder, forced me onto my knees. 'Just need summat to stand on. Go on, right down.'

On all fours, I could see what was coming and I wasn't happy. As Ralph planted one foot on my lower spine, I let out a low moan. Splaying my hands, I prayed my back would stand the strain. A second later, another groan made its way to the surface as my giant friend balanced all his weight on his new footstool.

'Ooh, Christ,' I muttered, trying not to sound pathetic.

'Shut yer face, I'll only be a second.'

I heard a thud followed by a bit of what my dad used to call 'rive and tear', a phrase employed for everything from splitting logs to carving the Sunday joint. A flurry of dust and plaster crashed to the floor, sprinkling my head and the surrounding area.

'Just one more good...' There was another thud

and more ripping, then what felt like a sackful of muck and rubbish crashed to the ground.

Ralph relieved me of my lowly position and helped me to my feet. 'There we are,' he said, rubbing his knuckles. 'What'd I say, eh? Amateurs.'

I looked down at the mess on the floor. Amidst all the lumps of plasterboard and dust, was a selection of what I supposed to be general building rubbish - small off-cuts of wood, crisp packets, half a mouldy sandwich and a few bent nails. But it was the five-inch length of angle bead that my friend was interested in.

'Now we've got tools.' He gave me a look that suggested I ought to congratulate him.

'That's great. What ye goin to do with it?'

Gathering up the nails, he picked out a few of the straightest ones and gave them to me. Then laying the torch down on the floor, he said, 'Start over there.' He pointed to the section he'd shown interest in earlier. 'Try and work the nails between the boards. I'll start on this bit.'

And so, on our knees, a few feet apart, we spent the next half hour or so trying to wedge nails in the almost non-existent gap between the planks Ralph assured me were most likely to yield an eventual escape route.

To pass the time, I told Ralph about my visit to Judy the Prostitute and Councillor White. He didn't have much to say on either subject, except for commenting on the poor quality of the beer in the North Sea.

I'd broken two fingernails and carved a nice chunk out of my thumb before we began to make progress. Ralph moved closer as he worked away at the gap until finally, sitting up, he reached for the section of angle bead. Laying it on the floor, he stood up and banged his foot down onto the metal, squashing the two sides together. Then, resuming his position next to me, muttered 'Moment of truth.'

Pushing one end of the device into the widest of the spaces we'd made between the planks, Ralph slipped off his shoe and started tapping it against the metal. At first, nothing happened but gradually it slid into the gap and as it did so, the wood either side seemed to give a little.

Slipping off his sock, I watched in mild amusement as Ralph wrapped it around the end of the angle bead and began to pull it towards himself.

'Quick! Slide the nails in.'

Amazingly, one of the floorboards had begun to lift away from its housing. I forced the nails into the newly created spaces, pressing down on them as much as I was able. A minute later Ralph was able to wedge the toe of his shoe into the gap.

'Now,' he said, standing up. 'This is the easy part.'

Crouching down on the opposite side to the gap, we grasped the now protruding edge of the plank and pulled. For a moment, nothing happened, then the wood creaked, protesting at our resolve to remove it.

'This time,' said Ralph, the ends of his fingers

white with the strain.

Renewing my hold, I tried to ignore the sharp edge as the wood dug into my flesh. I gave it my all. There was a woody screech and we fell backwards, the plank across our laps. Sitting up, I gazed at the hole it had left. Like this one, the ceiling of the room below had been plasterboarded, and similarly, the gaps between the joists were littered with rubbish.

'Lazy bastards,' said Ralph, pressing on the boards. Moving back, he took hold of the next plank along and gave it a tug. It came away easily. After that, it was a simple matter to pull up the next three, leaving only the ceiling below between us and the possibility of freedom.

Replacing his sock and shoe, Ralph balanced himself with a hand on my shoulder. He lifted his foot. A half dozen quick downward thrusts and the plasterboard gave way, revealing the room underneath.

Nevertheless, we still had to negotiate our way between the joists. In my case, I was able to slide my legs over the edge and through the hole without too much difficulty. After I dropped to the ground, I held the torch while Ralph squeezed himself through the gap. It took a bit of too-ing and fro-ing before he finally landed in a heap next to me.

It was only then that we were able to investigate our new surroundings.

We were standing in an empty warehouse - a high-roofed rectangular space with a huge shuttered door at one end and the obligatory fire escape at the other. Next to this was what looked like a small kitchen, while above us, the room that had until recently served as our prison, was attached to one wall. It was supported by four stout pillars and in the dim light I was able to make out the metal staircase that led up the wall to the door. A window looked out from the office onto the warehouse itself, so the other one must have been on the outside wall.

I was still considering the layout of the place when Ralph began rattling the shutters. 'Come on, Terry, we haven't got all bloody night.'

Hurrying over to join him, I hunted around for a light switch. Hitting the first one on a panel of switches, I was rewarded by a flickering above us, as two fluorescent tubes burst into life.

At the far side of the shutter was a looping chain that reached to the ceiling. Ralph pulled out the pin that kept it in place and started hauling away like a pirate on a promise. Immediately, the shutters began to rise. With the mechanism barely half way up, we slipped underneath and into the cool night air, allowing the shutter to clatter back to the ground.

The sky was still dark and the beginnings of the new day teased the horizon. I reckoned it must be about six in the morning. We'd been locked in for eight hours.

We stood for a moment taking in our new environment. A short driveway and parking area led down to an unfinished road. On either side were industrial units like ours. Unlike ours, most of the others had no roofs on. Glancing around the site, none of it looked familiar - there were no telltale landmarks, no burger vans whose owners might shed light on our geography. Even so, in one sense at least, I knew exactly where we were. Screwed to the corner of the industrial unit was a small wooden sign, bearing the image of a guard dog and declaring the security of the building to be maintained by a firm I'd heard of once too often - SAHB.

I looked at Ralph. 'Andersson.'

He nodded slowly.

The road to the left was a dead end, so we turned right and started walking.

Chapter 14

By the time we reached the edge of the industrial estate, we were no nearer guessing our location, but the fact we'd made it to a main road gave us a sort of spiritual, if not an actual, lift.

Ralph pointed to the left. 'Looks like a road sign up there.'

There was no footpath so we walked along the grass verge. As we got closer, the sky had lightened up enough to make out the names on the sign.

'Jesus, we're miles away.' I looked back down the way we'd come. 'Must be a couple of miles outside Killingworth.'

Ralph yawned. 'Aye, well, could be worse.' He started walking again. 'What time do your guys get in on a morning?'

For a minute I wondered who he meant by my 'guys,' then I realised. 'Office'll be open at half six. There's usually desk cover and one driver. The others turn up between seven and eight.'

'Just s'long as there's someone to come an pick us up.'

The walk to the nearest phone box was another mile down the road, past the roundabout and yet another new estate. While I made the call, Ralph went into the newsagents opposite. He came back with a bottle of water, a Mars bar and a Twix.

'Which d'ye want?'

'Not much of a choice,' I said, taking the Twix.

'It was either this or a two-day old cake-and-Sidney pie.'

We sat on the wall next to the phone box, staring into space. I fished in my pocket and pulled out the few coins I still had, and held them out.

Ralph shook his head. 'Nah, ye're fine. Owner's an old mate of mine.'

I nodded. 'Must've thought ye looked a bit of a sight?'

He looked down at himself and for the first time noticed the mess his trousers were in. He looked at me. 'Better than yours.'

We laughed, then fell into a genial silence.

Fat Barry's car was warm and reeked of bacon. 'Christ man, what the hell happened to you pair? Ye's been out shaggin sheep, or what?'

Ralph muttered something about a night on the tiles, which called a halt to Barry's questions, but the fat man's expression told me he wasn't satisfied. No doubt he'd do his nosy-parker act later.

It was surprisingly reassuring to sink into the fake-fur seats and close my eyes for a moment. As we set off, Barry turned the radio down and chuntered away about this and that, oblivious to the fact neither of us were listening.

We'd hit the outskirts of town before it occurred to me to tell him where I wanted to go.

'The cop shop? What the hell for?'

The thought of revealing what we'd been through

was too much to deal with, so I said it was a personal matter. He shut up after that and Ralph nodded a silent thank you.

Unsurprisingly, Ralph ducked out of my proposed meeting with Charis. He promised to sort the taxi fare out with Mrs Carver and said he'd be in touch shortly. I reminded him I didn't have a phone.

'Oh aye.' He climbed back into the car. 'I'll sort summat. See yer soon.'

It occurred to me, as I watched the taxi disappear round the corner, that Barry hadn't asked about Carol. Maybe that didn't mean anything in itself, but once again, I found myself wondering who I could trust.

The police station was one of those old-style red brick structures that look more like 1950s grammar schools than the headquarters of law and order. With the inevitable blue front door and matching windows, the only thing missing was a playground, but I guessed they'd have their own ways of passing time between arrests.

Inside, the place matched my expectations in both decor and atmosphere.

The desk sergeant was a seasoned professional with an air of undauntability about him, and seemed to fit right in with the olde worlde ambience. I told him I needed to speak to Inspector Brown as a matter of some urgency.

'This relating to an ongoing investigation is it, sir?'

'It is, yes.'

'Aye, well, she's not in yet. Ah can get the Duty Officer to come down if ye like?'

I shook my head. 'Really need to see Charis. I mean, Inspector Brown.'

If the sergeant drew any conclusions based on my over-familiarity, he kept them to himself. Making a show of turning to look at the clock on the wall, he said, 'Have to wait, then, won't ye?'

'Fine.' I spent a few minutes in the toilet wiping the blood and other crap off my face, then went back into reception and sat on one of the plastic chairs that lined one wall. I closed my eyes.

'Terry? Terry, wake up.'

I blinked and tried to focus. There was a hand on my shoulder. Charis stood over me. She was frowning in a way I interpreted as expressing moderate concern and I was pleased to see her elfin-like charm had reappeared. Behind her, DC Ramshaw hovered, a look of bemused distraction on his face. I wondered if he'd picked her up from home. Maybe she'd picked him up. Perhaps they'd come to mean more to each other than mere colleagues. I didn't think so - if he was shagging her, he'd have been grinning like the proverbial cat. Again.

'What's happened?'

I sighed. 'Long story.'

I finished my coffee and put the cup down.

Charis looked up from her notepad. She hadn't written anything. She glanced again at the printouts she'd picked up from her desk on the way through to the interview room. Whatever was on there, I guessed it wasn't good news.

'My problem, Terry, is that Sanjay Ahmed put a call in to Newcastle police last night. He reported a break-in at his property on Nugent Crescent and claimed the intruder was still on the premises. Two units attended and found signs of a struggle. Mr Ahmed gave a description, which, I have to say, matches you to a tee. He also claims the man who broke in has been hanging around the property for some time. According to him, the thief was alone.'

'Sorry, but have ye not been listenin?'

She tapped her pen on the table. 'You haven't told me anything useful yet.'

I coughed. Somehow, I'd expected her to listen, to take action, to do...something. 'Carol's missing. Christ knows what's happened to her. She could be...she could be dead or anything.'

She exchanged a glance with Ramshaw, who I noticed was looking very grown up. 'We've only got your word for that.'

I banged a hand on the table, making them both jump. 'For fuck's sake Charis, why won't you believe me?'

She leaned forward, her face hard and stony. 'Why the hell should I? You've been lying to me right from the start.'

I blinked. 'No, I've told ye —'

'Shite! That's what ye've told me, Terry. A total load of shite. Right from day one.' She swivelled her eyes to the right.

Following her gaze, I looked at Ramshaw and got the distinct impression that this was where the up-and-coming DC steps in with the punch line. I said, 'And I suppose you think the same, do ye?'

He stared straight back at me. 'What happened to the hockey stick?'

Turned out it was a sliver of wood that led them to the truth - one of several miniscule fragments they'd found embedded in Ronnie's face. You might think it'd be hard to match such a tiny item with an actual object, but no, not a problem at all. Not with the advances being made in technology. In fact, I wouldn't have been surprised if they had a 3D printer that could reproduce Sharon's hockey stick from scratch using only the tiniest of splinters.

Course, it hadn't been like that at all, not really. Although that tiny fragment had given them a clue, it had simply been a matter of the police talking to Sharon, and Sharon just happening to mention a particular item she'd left behind when she moved out. Yup. Good old detective work. Sherlock Fucking Holmes, eat your heart out.

So I had no choice. At least, that's what I'd tell myself later when the sloppy brown stuff would more than likely hit the apparatus with the rotating blades.

I told them about the argument with Frank, about

Bench Face and his bearded pal and about me and Carol's visits to Donny White and Judy the Spanx Queen. I didn't tell them about Ralph being with us the previous night - no point burning all my bridges.

And of course I told them about the blood on the hockey stick, the threats from Big Ronnie and the notes on the doors.

Charis let out the first of a series of heavy sighs before she eventually spoke.

'Tell me again about the notes.'

'Like what?'

'Like what you think they mean.'

I shrugged. 'I thought they were from Ronnie, or at least, I thought the first one was.'

She stared at her notepad. 'And they both said "Give it back?"'

'Pretty much.'

'So?'

I glanced at Ramshaw, who was now at the table, chin resting in his hands. 'Give what back?'

'I don't know.'

'Well someone must know. There has to be a motive.' Charis held up a finger. 'One: money.'

'Possibly,' I said. 'But it was Ronnie that owed me, so why would he send a reminder?'

'Good point.' She curled her finger back down, then it shot up again. 'The gear from your hackney cab?'

'He'd already sent me a couple of texts about that, but again, hardly summat to get in a tiz about.'

She kept the finger up and added another. 'Two: sex.'

I was tempted to say 'Not just now, pet,' but thought better of it. 'Look, this all started with Frank, so it must be about him, and Frank was having an affair, so...'

She nodded slowly. 'But why would Ronnie care?'

'Um...maybe Ronnie knew the woman Frank was seeing?'

She stared hard at me for a moment. 'Hang on...' She flicked through her pile of papers and pulled out a sheaf of forms. From where I sat, I could see they were photocopies of job sheets from the taxi office.

'We did a bit of diggin. Paul suggested we check through the records for the past six months, rather than just the two days we originally looked at.' She glanced across at Ramshaw. 'He picked these up last night.' Taking out two sheets, she passed them across the table. 'Here and here,' she said, indicating a couple of entries on each sheet, 'Ronnie picked up from the Hexagon and dropped off - supposedly - at Central Station in Newcastle.' She looked up. 'Ring any bells?'

'So he might have gone to Ahmed's place?'

She made a maybe-maybe-not gesture.' I'm not saying I believe all that bollocks about Ahmed, but if there's a connection..?'

I leaned forward and studied the sheets. 'What if Frank - for some reason - did some of Ronnie's regular pickups for him? Like, if Ronnie had a more important job lined up, he might have passed one or two on to another driver and Frank was about the only one he trusted.'

'Ye said Frank owed him money?'

'He did, but Frank was the first driver Ronnie took on - he'd been with the firm for ten years at least. Frank was there even before Ken got involved.'

'Okay. So if Frank found out something...' She shrugged.

'Like something involving this mysterious woman of his?'

She sat back and stared at the desk. 'Possibly.'

'None of this is helping find Carol.' I was trying not to sound irritated but it didn't quite work.

'We've got someone watching both Ahmed's place and Andersson's boat.'

'What about his house?'

She shook her head. 'He doesn't have a house.'

'He bloody does! Elise told me - it's out in the sticks somewhere.' I stared at her. 'I thought you'd checked all that?'

Her voice was steady. 'As far as we're aware, Mr Andersson spends all his spare time on his boat. There's no record of a house, no bills relating to property on his bank statements. Nothing.'

'He's got a house. Somewhere. I know he has.'

'And of course,' she added, 'we still haven't found Frank's car.'

When I left the police station, the first thing I saw was a black Volvo with tinted windows. It was parked across the road. The passenger side window buzzed down and Ralph cocked a finger at me.

'Got your car back, then?' I said.

He shook his head. 'Nah, this is Mrs Carver's. So if anythin happens to it, I'll be blamin you.'

As soon as I was inside, he took off towards the town centre.

'Where we goin?'

He glanced at me. 'To cast out the net.'

'What - fishin?'

'That's right, bonny lad - fishing for information.'

That sounded good, but I had more pressing concerns on my mind. 'We need to find Carol.'

Ralph pulled up at a T-junction and twisted round to look at me. 'Oh aye? Know where she is, do yer?'

'Well, no, not exactly...'

He nodded. 'That's why we're goin fishin.'

A minute later, we turned into Battlehill Terrace and pulled up outside one of the popular private hotels that were neither popular nor private. I'd done plenty pickups from the place in the past, but didn't have a Scooby about its present occupants.

'What we doing here?'

Ralph smiled. 'If I'm right, this'll be the fishing equivalent of cod and chips twice.'

I didn't bother trying to work out Ralph's metaphors, but guessed he knew what he was doing.

As the main door of the hotel was ajar, we walked straight in. The lobby boasted little in the way of welcoming decor and the walls bore the traces of several layers of paint and paper. I followed my large friend across the faded carpet to the stairs.

On the first floor, Ralph knocked on a door that led off the landing. A screechy voice called for us to hang on. I didn't recognise its owner until she opened the door.

Judy the Spanx Queen looked up at Ralph and sighed in a way that suggested some past acquaintance. She blinked several times like she'd got something in her eye, then pulled her nightie around herself. I was glad it wasn't of the see-through variety. Her fingers fidgeted with the buttons.

She turned to me. 'What now?'

I was about to speak but Ralph jumped in first.

'A little bird told iz ye had some information. About a job ye passed on.'

Her eyes swivelled up to Ralph, but her face still pointed at me. Her mouth opened. 'Erm...Ah divvent think so...'

Ralph moved so quickly it made me jump. Grabbing Judy's arm, he twisted it behind her, prompting a yelp of pain.

'Christ man! What the fuck ye doin?'

Ralph sprang forward, propelling her backwards into the flat. I followed in his wake as he pushed her along the short passageway and into a room at the end.

Judy wriggled free of his grasp and jumped back, but Ralph had stopped in the doorway, blocking off any means of escape. Peering over his shoulder, I looked into the room and was surprised to find myself face to face with a familiar young man of dubious origin.

'Oh, crap. What da fuck you doin here, man?'

My Jamaican Cockney friend was naked except for a strategically placed cushion, which he held over his dangly bits.

'Might ask you the same question,' I said.

Ralph stepped forward and turned to me. 'Ye know this fucker?'

I told him about our previous meeting in the lane behind Ahmed's house and the fact he was acquainted with the man called Horse.

Gesturing to the unclothed fellow on her sofa, Ralph turned to Judy. 'Client, is he?'

'Client? Cheeky bastard. What ye think I am?'

'I know what you are, bonny lass. Just answer the question.'

Judy shook her head as if to rid herself of the accusation.

'Who gave you the job?'

She raised her chin in an act of further defiance, but in doing so, her eyes flicked towards her companion.

Ralph caught the look and a smile spread over his features. 'Thought as much. Now, young man...'

Judy seemed about to object but said nothing

more.

Moving forward, Ralph reached into his jacket and pulled out what looked like a piece of rolled-up leather. Standing directly in front of Judy's gentleman friend, he made a show of unrolling it, revealing a number of highly-polished items slotted into neat little pockets. Selecting a pair of secateurs, he passed the tool roll to me.

'Whatcha doin wiv dat, bro?'

'I'll ask the questions,' said Ralph. 'What's your name, son?'

For a moment, it looked as if belligerence might get the better of the young lothario, but then he shrugged and said, 'Barney.'

Ralph glanced at Judy and she gave a slight nod.

'Okay, Barney,' he said, brandishing the shears. 'We'd like answers to several questions.'

Barney made a face. 'What - ye goin to cut ma cock off?' He grinned and shook his head. 'Nah. Judy's told me about you. You ain't the type.'

This seemed like a stupid thing to say, given the particularly mean look on Ralph's face and the nearness of the cutters to Barney's scrotum, but the upturned chin and downturned mouth gave him a strangely heroic demeanour. I almost admired his bravado.

Ralph's face seemed to visibly cool, as if it had somehow metamorphosed into a block of marble. He stood for a long time, staring down at the young man, eyes hard and wide. Then he shrugged and nodded. 'You know what? You're right - I'm no

Shylock, and in any case I don't reckon I'd get a pound of flesh off that scraggy bit of black puddin ye've got there. But then, it's not your flesh I'm interested in.' And with that he jumped forward and grabbed a handful of Barney's dreadlocks.

The young man's reaction was delightful. Abandoning both the cushion and his vulnerability, he jumped up, pulling at Ralph's arm, trying to steer it away from his precious coiffure.

'No, man, not that...'

Judy was trembling, her feet shuffling forward. She seemed about to jump into the fray, but I moved between her and Barney, allowing Ralph the space he needed to play his winning hand. A second later, Barney was on his back on the sofa, Ralph's knee on his chest and a hank of hair between the blades of the shears.

'Right. You ready to answer my questions now, son?'

Chapter 15

Back in the car, Ralph slipped the unused shears into their pocket and tied up the tool roll. He slid the key into the ignition then looked at me.

'Go on then - ask.'

'Ask what?'

He frowned. 'You okay, Terry? Look like you're in shock.'

I let out a long breath and shook my head. 'Just wasn't what I was expectin.'

He sniffed and eased the car away from the kerb. 'Yeah, I know.' After a moment he said, 'Which way?'

'Towards the golf club.'

He nodded and took the next left.

I stared out the window, pondering how to approach things. Whichever way our next encounter went, there were going to be consequences - the sort of consequences I didn't want to think about. I decided to leave the details to chance and occupy my mind with something less demanding.

I said, 'Go on then - how d'you know Judy?'

'What makes ye think I know her?'

'Bloody obvious.'

'An there's me thinkin I was being inscrutable.' He coughed. 'She's me mam's sister. Usual story. Got in with a bad lot, started doin drugs at fifteen and it all went downhill from there.' His eyes told me this was as much as I was going to get, so I let it go.

It amazed me how towns like this one seemed to cultivate multiple layers of overlapping relationships, each one linked to another and yet another, to the point where I sometimes thought the whole town was one big, sprawling, interrelated clan, complete with all the back-biting, snidey, hypocritical cattiness most families have. Except with this one, there was always one more skeleton lurking in the wardrobe with yet another sordid secret waiting to be exposed.

Just past the clubhouse, I directed Ralph to take a left onto the Farmway. It was one of those Leech-built estates that were thrown up in the late Sixties to replace pit houses and welfare cottages, with the promise of ridding its residents of the curse of outside toilets. Trouble was, unlike the dwellings they were meant to be replacing, these houses weren't built to last and cracks started appearing within a few months of the first punters moving in. Now, half of them were up for sale and the other half were home to folk who still thought property was worth hanging on to.

Like many similar communities, Mr Leech had pinched a few ideas from the New Town developments and factored in areas for growth. Consequently, most of these estates had their own shops, a pub or two and if they were really lucky, a community centre. But it wasn't the wellbeing of the community I was interested in.

Taking a right past the handful of shops, I told Ralph to pull up on the opposite side of the road. We both turned to look at the not-so-modern edifice that sat on a quarter-acre of land between the two halves of the estate. The place looked like it had been modelled on one of those quaint, timber-built country churches in Virginia - the ones that are always painted white and look far too good for sinners and repentant souls. Unfortunately, the builder had utilised several tons of the pale yellow bricks so beloved of northern collieries. I dare say it must have looked okay to begin with, but to my mind, it'd never resembled anything but a monument to dead miners. And not a very good one, at that.

I got out the car and looked up at the scaffolding. A couple of swarthy-looking guys were leaning on the railing at the top, watching us.

'One of them?' said Ralph.

'No.' I walked round the side of the building and found the main door. It was already open, held in place by a pile of bricks.

Even allowing for the huge arched windows, the scaffolding and layers of polythene covering the walls outside had so diminished the natural light, that there was a gloominess to the interior. Here and there cables hung over the rafters, with light bulbs dangling from the ends, illuminating the central section of the main hall. Most of the pews had been ripped out and the initial framework of stud walls erected, the plan presumably to separate the space into individual apartments. To the right was a door leading to a side room where I imagined the clergy would've helped themselves to wine and biscuits. Now the space was piled high with bags of plaster.

At the far end of the hall, through the maze of pine joists, three familiar faces looked up from their task. The one with the beard dropped the sheet of plasterboard he was holding, letting it crash to the floor. I waved a cheery hello at his friends.

Directly in front of us, a makeshift desk had been rigged up over the top of a couple of the remaining pews, where a man in a waxed jacket was poring over a series of diagrams laid out across the top. He straightened up and glared at Monkey Boy.

'What the hell you doing? You know how much I pay for those?'

None of them spoke, though all three made vague pointing gestures, indicating that they were no longer alone. It was only then that David turned round and saw us.

'Terry? What a nice er...' He frowned and looked at his watch. 'What you doing here?'

'Ye said pop in any time. So we have.' My voice came out sounding less composed than I'd've liked, and there was a note of something close to panic that surprised me. Realising my fists were clenched, I willed myself to relax, to take a breath.

My sister's husband cleared his throat and gave a strained laugh. 'Aye, well obviously I didn't mean just *any* time.'

I nodded towards my friend. 'This is Ralph, a mate of mine.'

Ralph raised an eyebrow, but said nothing.

David jumped to a conclusion and shook his head. To Ralph he said, 'Sorry mate, I haven't any jobs going just now.' He gave me a pained look. 'Terry...'

I held up a hand, only too aware of the tremor in my fingers. 'We're not here about jobs.'

He inclined his head and for a moment I thought he might be about to laugh, then it seemed that a flicker of doubt skated across his face. He coughed and shook his head again. 'Ye've lost me, Terry. What's this about?'

I pointed to his employees. 'Don't ye know? I'm sure your minions do.'

David turned his head towards them and tried another laugh, but the colour had drained from his face, the way it does in movies when the villain of the piece realises he's in the shit.

'Look, er...I'm sure we can sort this out...'

Ralph stepped forward. 'In here.' He took hold of David's arm and headed for the side room.

I glanced over at Beardy, Benchy and the Less Ugly One, but it was obvious they had no intention of getting involved. Not this time.

I closed the door behind me. David turned to face us, his back to a pile of British Gypsum bags. Ralph and I stood opposite him in the small space. There was nowhere to go.

'Now look...'

'No, you look.' I held up a finger, but the tremor was still there. Typically, my bottom lip decided to join in as well. I closed my mouth, clamping my teeth shut, striving to get control of myself. Thankfully, Ralph was more than up to the task in hand.

'Ye put your boys onto Terry.' It wasn't a question.

David licked his lips. 'Look, I only found out this morning they were involved, I had no idea.'

'Aye, right.'

'Really, Terry, you have to believe me. You've got to understand –'

'They had a gun, David, a fuckin gun.'

His eyes went like saucers. 'Jesus. I didn't –'

I stepped forward and grabbed the lapel of his jacket. 'Don't make on ye didn't know. How d'ye think fuckface in there got a hole in his foot?' I gave him a shake and pushed him back against the bags.

'Terry, man, I didn't know it was them.' His face had regained some of its colour and was now heading toward the beetroot spectrum. 'I gave the job to –'

He stopped abruptly, as if it'd suddenly dawned on him what he was saying.

'Go on,' I said. 'Ye gave the job to who, exactly?'

He dropped his head. When it came, his voice was barely a whisper. 'This Jamaican guy I know. Call him Brian, or Barney, or something...' He gave a pathetic shrug. 'How was I to know he'd farm it out to those guys in there? I mean, my own workers! It's farcical.' He shook his head and laughed harshly. 'You couldn't make it up.'

'Aye, well,' I said. 'Didn't have to, did ye?'

'Look, Terry...'

'Thing is, Davey Boy,' said Ralph, 'it still comes down to you, doesn't it? So, what we're goin to do...' He placed a hand on my chest, pushing me gently to one side. 'Is go into the removal business.' Slowly and deliberately, he took out the tool roll and extracted the secateurs.

David stared at him. 'What? You're not serious?'

Ralph glanced at me. 'Ye up to this, bonny lad? It's fine if ye're not.'

I nodded and muttered, 'I'm up to it.'

Ralph seized David's right hand. 'You take the other one.'

Moving forward, I pressed myself against my brother-in-law, grasping his left arm and holding it away from his body so he couldn't move. It occurred to me that with his arms outstretched like this, we were unwittingly creating a kind of unsophisticated crucifixion. I would've laughed if the circumstances had been different.

David began to thrash about, pulling at my arms, struggling to free himself. Changing position, I braced my feet to gain a better stance. But still he heaved this way and that, kicking out at my legs. Our chests pressed together and the unexpected heat from his body was disconcerting. A wave of nausea washed over me and there was a bad taste in my mouth.

'Get the fuck off me, now!'

Holding him firm, I glanced at Ralph for guidance. He clearly had no difficulty keeping David's other hand still. He gave me a sharp, questioning look. *Was this what I wanted?* I nodded.

David thrust his chest out, letting out a low groan, then slumped forwards, exhausted. He turned to me, his eyes pleading. 'Terry, man, there's no need for any of this, is there? We can work something out.' His voice was hoarse and I could smell cigarettes on his breath. I wondered if Jessie knew he smoked.

'I'm sure we can –'

He stopped as the secateurs bit into his little finger.

David didn't scream. Rather, he let out a sort of feeble half-yelp, a quiet objection.

Ralph maintained his position, David's wrist gripped firmly in his meaty hand, the newly-assaulted little finger nestled between the blades of the secateurs, blood dripping from the cut.

'Now,' he said. 'As ye can see, it's only superficial, no real damage done. Yet. But I'll easy cut it off if ye like. No bother at all. All it needs is a little squeeze.' He grinned. 'And then there were nine.'

David's eyes were so wide I thought they might actually pop out of his head. 'Don't cut it off, please don't...'

'Then tell us what we want to know.' Ralph's voice was soft, almost kindly.

David swallowed noisily.

'All right. I've got this contract, see, renovating old buildings. It's part of a new development to create sustainable dwellings for older people. You know the sort of thing, low rent and –'

'Aye, whatever,' said Ralph. 'Get on with it.'

David nodded vigorously. 'It's worth a lot of money but there are deadlines and massive fines if I don't get the work done on time.' He paused, glanced at me, then dropped his eyes. 'I was told you were interfering. That I had to...discourage you. Somehow.'

'Told by who?'

He looked up. 'I can't say.'

I let go the breath I'd been holding. 'Sven Andersson.'

'What?' David frowned, then seemed to give himself a bit of a shake. He nodded quickly. 'Yes, he's the main investor, see? Along with Sanjay Ahmed and a few others.' He was into his stride now, words tumbling out. He shrugged.

'So it was Sven who told you to sort me out?'

David's face scrunched up and he looked away. 'Pretty much.'

'Pretty much? Either it was or it wasn't.'

'It was a phone call.'

'From him?'

He seemed less certain now. 'One of his cronies.'

I shook my head. 'Bastard.'

Ralph loosened his grip on David's finger but not before promising recriminations if the rest of our questions weren't answered.

Unfortunately, as it turned out, my dear relation wasn't part of the inner workings of the Andersson gang, so his involvement amounted to little more than doing what he was told in return for hefty backhanders. He maintained he'd had nothing to do with the caravan fire or anything else, except the business at the farmhouse. It all sounded a little absurd and I struggled to see why he'd have got involved with the Anderssons in the first place. Surely it couldn't be just for the money? But then something else occurred to me.

'What ye goin to tell Jess?'

His face hit the deck. 'Oh Christ, you won't mention this to her, will you, Terry?'

I shook my head. 'No, I won't. *You* will.'

He half-laughed. 'No, really. You don't know her.'

'I think I do, actually.' I rested a hand on his shoulder and noticed my tremor had disappeared. 'Tell you what - you tell us something that's actually useful, like where Carol is, or who killed Ronnie, etc etc...and I'll see what I can do.'

His mouth dropped open. 'What's happened to Carol?'

I wasn't convinced he didn't know, but had to admit that he did a pretty good impression of looking surprised when I related the events of the previous night.

'There's a place you can try where they might be keeping her. It's a house up the West End, on Nugent Crescent.'

'No, we've been there,' I started.

David waved his injured hand. 'No, not that one. I mean the one next door.'

I looked at Ralph. 'Next door?'

David nodded. 'That's where they...' He stopped and looked off to one side, as if trying to recall what it was he'd been about to say. I had the distinct impression he thought he'd said too much.

Ralph leaned forward and grasped David's injured finger, twisting it backwards. 'That's where they what?'

David squealed and pulled his hand away, tucking it under his arm. 'That's where they keep the girls.'

'Oh, fuck.' I lashed out and caught him around the neck. 'And you knew about this? You fuckin knew?' My hand began to tighten.

Ralph took hold of my arm. 'Divvent kill him, Terry, or your sister'll kill you.'

This was true. I let go.

David doubled up, gasping for breath and holding his neck. After a moment, he managed to straighten up. 'I've never been there, Terry, you have to believe me.'

'So how d'you know about the girls?'

'I don't, really. Just something I overheard while having a drink with Ahmed. One of his men called him and Ahmed said something about the new woman they'd got hold of and that she'd be going in with the other whores next door.'

Chapter 16

We shoved David in the back of the car and took the coast road to Newcastle. No-one spoke until we were on Westgate Road and within a mile of our destination, by which time the rain had started again. I'd have preferred total darkness to this autumnal half-light, so was thankful when the skies began to take on a suitably gloomy outlook that seemed more appropriate to our mission.

As we approached the turn-off, I remembered my car and directed Ralph to the bottom end of the road. The Nissan was exactly where I'd left it.

'Where ye going?' said Ralph as I jumped out.

With a hand already in my pocket, I remembered I didn't have the keys. If I'd thought about it, we could've picked up the spare set from the taxi office, but we'd been in too much of a rush to think logically. Trying my luck, I pressed down on the boot lock, giving it what I hoped was the magic thump, but it stayed locked. Moving round to the driver's side window, I peered through the glass and amazingly, the keys were right there in the ignition. Maybe the bad guys had hoped it would get nicked and save them the trouble of getting rid of it.

I found what I wanted and relocked the car.

'What the fuck ye doin with that?' asked Ralph, as I climbed in beside him.

'Think it looks real?'

'Looks bloody real to me,' he said, leaning away from me.

I shuffled round in my seat and aimed the Luger at David's head. 'Bang, fucking, bang.'

'Jesus, Terry, be careful!' His hands shot up in front of his face.

'Aye, it's funny havin a gun pointed at ye, isn't it?' I shoved the weapon inside my jacket out of sight. 'Don't worry, it's only a replica. Got it off Bummer Harris. Just in case.'

We turned around and parked up on the main road, then walked back down to Nugent Crescent. David limped along behind us, still clutching his injured hand.

Reaching the green door, we stopped outside the next house along.

'This it?'

David shrugged. 'How would I know?'

I stared at him. 'Well, is it or isn't it?'

'He said it was next door. That's all I know.'

Ralph rolled his eyes. 'Right, only one way to find out.' He started up the path. Grabbing his sleeve, I pulled him back.

'Wait. What if it's the wrong one?'

'If it's the wrong one it doesn't matter, does it?' and before I could object, he'd knocked on the door.

A moment later, it swung open and a wizened face peered out.

'Yes dear?'

Ralph cleared his throat. 'Sorry to bother ye and

that, but I wondered if Mr Ahmed was here?'

The old woman shook her head. 'No pet, ye want number 37.' She smiled and nodded then closed the door.

We backtracked past the green door to the next house along.

'Second time lucky, eh?' said Ralph, starting up the path again. He banged on the door, then glancing over his shoulder muttered, 'Better get your gun out.'

I took up a position beside him, holding the Luger out of sight inside my jacket. When the door opened, it seemed like everything stopped.

My lips went through the motions of forming a sentence, but no sound came out.

To be fair, the expression on Donny White's face showed he hadn't expected us any more than we'd expected him. His mouth opened and closed a few times, as if worked by a thread. Finally, he murmured, 'Oh, it's you.'

For a moment, I was too stunned to do anything, then as Donny came to his senses and tried to shut the door, I barged past him, pushing him back against the wall.

'Who else is here?' I kept my voice low and stuck the Luger under his chin.

'The lads are in the kitchen.' He raised a shaking finger and pointed along the passageway.

'And the women?'

He closed his eyes, then nodded his head. 'Downstairs.'

Ralph closed the door quietly, then with Donny in front and David bringing up the rear, we headed towards the sound of voices at the back of the house.

My tremor had come back with a vengeance and my hand was shaking so much I could hardly keep hold of the weapon. I whispered in the fat man's ear. 'Downstairs, ye said?'

He nodded and opened a door on the left.

Glancing inside, I saw a flight of stone steps leading down into what must be the cellar. I nudged Donny with the gun. He began to descend the stairs, and I was grateful he had the sense to do so quietly.

At the foot of the stairs was another door, bolted top and bottom. Donny knelt down and eased the bolt out. The top one proved to be a little awkward and squeaked as he slid it backwards.

I turned to Ralph. 'You stay here. I don't want anyone shutting us in.'

He nodded and reached into his outside jacket pocket, pulling out a small cosh. 'Mind, if they've got guns, we're fucked.' He grinned.

I pushed the door inwards. It opened into a short passage leading to another door at the end, this one unlocked. As I opened the second door, I heard a gasp from inside. Pushing slowly forwards, I looked in.

The room was about fifteen feet square, with four single divan beds in a line against one wall. A small lamp sat on a cabinet opposite. No other furniture was in the room apart from a dilapidated commode in the far corner.

Carol was crouched on the end of the nearest bed, her hands and feet bound. Two other women sat on the other beds, similarly tied. I crossed the room in three quick strides and pulled the gag out of her mouth.

'Terry!' Her voice was hoarse and tears were already streaming down her face. I glanced round. 'David - come on. Move!' My fingers were shaking almost uncontrollably as I struggled to undo the knots.

David moved to the other girls and began pulling at the ropes.

I checked on Donny and saw he hadn't moved from the doorway. 'You as well - *do* something.' Reluctantly, he shuffled over and began unfastening the third girl's bonds.

It seemed to take an age to free them all, but eventually we got them on their feet. I guessed that the other two women were in their early twenties. They had an eastern European look to them and were dressed in outdoor clothes with shoes on their feet. Carol still wore the same clothes she'd had on when I last saw her. As soon as she was free, she wrapped her arms around my neck.

'Thought I was never goin to see yer again,' her sobs muffled as she blubbed into my collar.

I took hold of her shoulders and held her away from me. 'Plenty time for that later. We need to get out of here, all right?'

She nodded, tearfully.

I picked up the strands of rope, thinking they might come in useful.

Ralph was peering up the staircase. He held a hand out to silence us. 'Don't move.'

We stood stock still for a long moment until he made a come-hither motion with his fingers. 'Dead quiet, mind.'

Carol's hand was in mine and she held on tight as we began our ascent. Ralph moved cautiously up the stairs, halting every other step to listen. By the time we got to the top, my legs were like jelly.

On our way down, Ralph had shut the door. Now he leaned against it, listening. He turned round, his voice barely audible. 'We get the women outside. David can take them to the car.' He wagged a finger at me. 'Me and you need to have a look in the kitchen.'

My heart sank. Even though I was just as keen as he was to find out who was behind all this, I really didn't want to be coming face to face with them at this particular moment in time. Nevertheless, I nodded.

Easing the door open, Ralph looked out, then opened it fully and waved Carol and me into the passageway. We headed for the front door, the others close behind.

It was only when the outside air hit my face that I felt a sense of relief. I stood by the door breathing deeply until all three women were on the path. Ralph gave David the keys to the Volvo.

'Give us ten minutes. If we're not there, get the

hell out of here, okay?'

David nodded and led the women out onto the pavement.

Carol's eyes were on mine, but I waved her away. 'Go on. Go.'

We waited until they were a good way up the road before going back into the house.

Donny was standing by the door. 'Sorry,' he muttered.

'Aye, so am I.'

Ralph put a hand on Donny's shoulder and gave him a gentle squeeze. 'How many are there?'

Donny shrugged. 'Three, maybe. Unless anyone else's come in the back way.'

'Excellent.' I looked at Ralph. 'What's the plan?'

He leaned down towards me. 'We'll leave the front door open, just in case we need to do a runner. Your mate here can go first.' He gave Donny a hard stare. 'You give us away and I'll fucking plant ye, all right?'

Donny nodded.

Moving forward, the fat man led us along to the door at the end. This opened into what, in any normal house, would have been the lounge, though the way the chairs were set out, it looked more like a dentist's waiting room. Obviously, this was for clients, while they waited for their appointments.

At the other end of the room was another door. Donny took hold of the handle. The voices were louder now and I reckoned Donny was right - there were at least three of them.

Ralph glanced at me, then gave Donny the nod.

Donny opened the door and stepped inside.

Somehow, I'd expected to recognise the men in the kitchen, but the three faces that turned towards us were all new to me.

The two youngest guys, both Asian, were furthest away. One was stirring what smelled like curry in a big saucepan on the stove. The other was in the midst of pouring wine into three mugs.

The man nearest the door looked about my age. He was perched on a chair the wrong way round, arms folded across its back. He grinned at Donny then jumped up on realising their doorman wasn't alone.

'Fuck!' He grabbed something from the kitchen table and I saw his arm swing back. But Ralph was quicker and shot forward, bringing his cosh down across the man's head. The wine bottle fell to the ground, spilling its contents across the linoleum.

The two guys behind were slower to react and I was past Ralph and pointing the gun at them before they had actually moved a muscle.

With the first man on the ground, cradling his injured bonce, his friends seemed less keen to try their mettle, and simply stood there, hands at their sides.

'Step away from the curry,' I said to the one by the cooker. His mate put the bottle down and moved back.

'See?' said Ralph, 'This is what happens when ye drink on duty.'

I waved the gun. 'That's right. Backs against the wall.' They did as I asked, glancing at each other. 'And don't even think about tryin anythin.'

Ralph planted a foot on the older guy's neck. 'Where are the others?'

The man on the floor muttered something about them being out of town.

'Oh well,' said Ralph. 'Just means you lot'll have to take the rap, eh?'

It took us a few minutes to tie them up with the ropes from the cellar. I paid special attention to Donny, whose face was now whiter than a shade of pale. When we were certain there was no chance of any of them escaping, I used the house phone to call the police.

David, Carol and the other two women were in the Volvo. As the three of us crossed to the car, I could see flashing lights in the distance. When the boys and girls in blue were close enough, I stepped into the road and waved them down.

It was something o'clock in the morning and I was back at the police station sitting on the same plastic chair I'd occupied the previous day. Ralph sat next to me, having decided it was probably less hassle to contribute what he knew to the tale, than it would be if he simply waited for the cops to come to him.

I was onto my third cup of powdered machine-issue coffee when Charis reappeared. She jerked her head at me and I followed her through to the same room I'd been in before. With any luck, the result this time round would be more satisfactory.

Ramshaw was sitting at the table. He nodded and gave me one of those smiles he'd been working on.

'So,' said Charis, when she'd settled herself again. 'Turns out ye were right all along. Mostly.'

'I won't say I told ye so.'

'That's good, because there's still a heap of stuff that doesn't add up.'

I listened while she explained about the two Polish women and how they'd been employed initially at the Hexagon before being invited to 'help out' at one of Mr Ahmed's parties. Apparently, they were only a small part of the resources Ahmed laid on for his business associates. A means of keeping the wheels of industry running smoothly, or some such shit like that.

'We caught up with Ahmed and his wife at a business dinner in Gateshead. They and their cronies are in custody in Newcastle, but none of them are admitting much.'

'And Councillor White?'

Charis sighed. 'Waiting for his solicitor, but I expect he'll only admit to a few backhanders and a bit of hanky panky on the side.'

'What about Andersson?'

'That's one of the things they're not admitting. Without a confession, we've nothing to tie Sven or Elise Andersson to anything connected to Ahmed.'

'You're joking? What about David? It was the Anderssons who told him to stop me interfering.'

She shook her head. 'Apparently not. We've spoken to David Seaton at length and according to him the order was given over the phone by a man. But even if we could trace the call to Sven, we'd be hard pushed to prove he actually made the call.'

'Oh for God's sake. There must be something you can do?' I looked at Ramshaw, who so far hadn't contributed to the discussion. 'Ye still haven't found Frank's car, have ye?'

The DC shrugged. 'It could be anywhere.'

'Well what about the Polish women? Did either of them know Frank?'

'Again, no. Or if they did, they're not saying. And given what they went through, it's hardly surprising.' He paused. 'I know it doesn't sound like it, but...' He glanced at Charis. 'We are grateful for your intervention. If you hadn't got into the house when you did, Christ knows what might have happened.'

Charis nodded. 'You'll be able to see Carol shortly - she's just going over her formal statement.'

I dropped my head. The whole thing was ridiculous. We were no closer to finding out what happened to Frank or learning who killed Ronnie than we'd been a week ago.

We sat for a few minutes in silence, then Charis said, 'Why don't you go and wait for Carol? She won't be long.'

DC Ramshaw took me back through to reception where I sat down next to Ralph. He'd succumbed to the powdered coffee.

'All right?' he said.

'Suppose.'

'Anything ye don't want me to tell them?'

I shook my head.

'Presume ye didn't mention the you-know-what?'

In the excitement, I'd forgotten about the gun. 'It's under the passenger seat in your car.'

'No bother.'

Leaning forward, I rested my elbows on my knees, my head in my hands. It felt as though the whole thing was over and done, like I could just forget about it all and go home. But I couldn't. Not without finding the last few pieces of the puzzle.

'By the way,' Ralph leaned over and handed me a mobile phone. 'Meant to give ye that earlier. Complements of Mrs C.'

'Thanks. I'll treasure it.'

Carol emerged a few minutes later, looking miraculously undishevelled considering her ordeal. She sank down next to me and leaned her head on my shoulder.

'Don't have to go home, do I?'

'Don't have to,' I said. 'Come to mine if ye like?'

She nodded. 'Aye. I like.'

We left Ralph waiting for his turn with Charis and headed for home. If there'd been anything open, we'd have collected a takeaway and a bottle of wine on the way, but there wasn't.

The flat looked just how I'd left it, or rather, just how someone else had left it the last time I was there. I deposited Carol in the living room, found a packet of Custard Creams and a bottle of Pinot Grigio I'd forgotten I had. The wine was poured and the biscuits were shared but the effort of eating and drinking was a little too much and we shuffled off to bed shortly after seven o'clock in the morning.

I hadn't thought to ask Carol if she wanted to sleep alone, but as neither of us had the strength to get undressed, it hardly mattered. I switched off the light and turned onto my side, watching Carol's eyelids fluttering. I gazed at her for as long as I could, striving to keep my eyes open for just another few minutes, but the effort was too much and I could do nothing more than give in to fatigue and join my companion in sleep.

Chapter 17

I awoke to the smell of pizza.

At some point during the night, I must have cast off some of my clothes, since I was now only wearing socks and trousers. I stripped off, pulled on my dressing gown and followed the smell through to the kitchen.

'I was just goin to call yer.' Carol gave me a wide smile and shared the pizza between two plates.

'Pepperoni? For breakfast?'

'I'd have made porridge but there's no milk. I've got the coffee on. Black, of course.'

'Of course.'

She was wearing one of my old T-shirts and a pair of socks. Picking up the plates, she took them through to the living room and put them on the coffee table.

I sat on the sofa and tucked in. According to the clock, it was almost four in the afternoon. I felt like I should be doing something, but couldn't think what that something might be.

We didn't speak much, each of us concentrating on eating. Eventually, Carol patted her tummy and declared breakfast over.

'So what now?'

I shook my head. 'No idea.'

'Well, I think we should have a shower first.'

I blinked. 'Together?'

She rolled her eyes. 'No, Terry, not together. Just cos we've slept in the same bed doesn't mean I want ter get naked with you.' She looked away, then giving me a coy sideways glance, added, 'Not yet, anyway.'

It wasn't much of a plan. In fact it wasn't a plan at all. Sitting in the car round the corner from the taxi rank waiting for a certain someone to come along, seemed like a bit of a George Formby long shot, but it was all we had.

Carol leaned over the back seat and patted my shoulder. 'What'll we do if nothing happens?'

'Go back to bed.'

'Tell ye what - if we catch them, we'll go back to bed. All right?'

I would've laughed but a familiar face caught my attention first. 'There.' I hunched down and pointed along the line of waiting taxis to the woman climbing into Fat Barry's car.

'That's her!' Carol shook the back of my seat. 'Come on Terry, get after her.'

I pulled away from the kerb at the same time as Peado Pete, so we had the advantage that Barry wouldn't have a clear view of us in his rear mirror. Although, with Elise Andersson in the back of his cab, I guessed his eyes wouldn't be on the road.

We followed at a steady pace as they turned onto the Esplanade and headed towards Tynemouth. They could be going to the Hexagon, but I was hoping it'd be somewhere more significant.

I realised we weren't going to the restaurant when Barry took a right past the swimming pool. For a minute, I wondered if he was going round in a circle. Maybe he'd sussed we were following, though why he should be concerned about that was anyone's guess.

'Where's she going?' said Carol, her chin on the back of the seat.

'I'll tell you when we get there.'

We were heading out of town. Maybe Elise just wanted a nice drive in the country, but I doubted it.

I dropped back a little as we hit the quieter roads - it didn't seem likely Elise would be watching out the back window, but I didn't want to get too cocky. A couple of miles further on, a familiar house came into view and I was more than a little surprised when Barry's car turned left onto what I knew was a narrow winding road that led past several houses and a farm.

'Shite.'

'What?'

'I know where they're going.' I pulled up a little way past the turn off, just far enough so I could still see Barry's car through the trees. There was no way I could follow him without being seen.

'What's along there?' said Carol.

'It's a house Ralph went to.'

She frowned. 'Ralph? You don't think..?'

'Don't know what to think, to be honest.' Whatever I might be thinking about it, I couldn't stay where I was, so I chucked the car into gear and set off up the road. A hundred yards further on, I pulled into a farm track and turned the car around. Edging forward, we could just about see the other turn-off. I reached into the glove compartment and took out the binoculars. The view wasn't bad, but I'd only have a couple of seconds to check who was in the car, and that was supposing Barry came back the way he'd come. And if he came out and turned left, he'd see us for sure.

As it happens, my fat friend did appear two minutes later and pulled up at the junction. I could see him easily through the binocs. Somewhat unsurprisingly, he'd stopped to stuff his face with chocolate. Once his gob was full, he pulled forward, allowing me a good look into the back of the car, and unless Elise Andersson was crouching down or lying dead on the back seat, she was no longer his passenger.

I gave it a few minutes for Barry to quit the scene, then hoofed it down to the turn off and hammered up to the lay-by. I slowed down as we sailed past and noted the BMW was parked at the front of the house.

There were no signs of life, but I didn't want to risk anyone seeing us, so I continued along the road for a minute, looking for somewhere to hide. About half a mile on, the surrounding woodland opened out into a space where piles of logs had been stacked up. I stopped the car and reversed in.

We got out and looked back down the lane.

'There, ye can still see the house.'

Carol took my hand. 'Ye sure about this, Terry? Maybe we should wait til it's dark?'

I looked up at the sky. It had clouded over again and would probably be dark enough for what we wanted in an hour or so. 'Yeah, you're probably right. Don't want to push our luck, do we?'

We hung around for a while, watching what little we could see of the house. As the rain started again, I reasoned it'd give us enough cover to approach unseen. Besides, there were plenty of trees around. So long as we were careful, we'd be fine.

Keeping well over to the side, we made our way along the lane. As we got closer, it seemed sensible to get in among the trees, just in case anyone came past.

We pushed into the woods. There were no paths, so it was slow progress stomping through the wet undergrowth towards our target. Within ten minutes, we were almost at the edge of the woods where they backed onto the house. A hundred or so yards more and we'd have an unobstructed view.

'Terry, what we goin to do when we get there?' Carol was clinging to my hand like she was scared to let go.

'I don't know. Maybe we'll be able to see something. You know - something that'll give us a clue, or summat.'

'Ye'd make a great detective,' she said, grinning.

It was quite gloomy now and I was glad to see several lights coming on inside the house. At least we wouldn't be floundering around in the dark.

'I want to get further round, so we can see the back of the place properly.' We pushed on, moving deeper into the woods, keeping enough trees between us and the house to avoid being seen if anyone came out.

Forging ahead, and concentrating on the task in hand, I hadn't looked up for a few minutes, so when we reached the area I'd been heading for, it came as a shock to be awarded an unencumbered view of the rear of the house.

There was no garage or garden shed, only a heaped-up mound at the far side of the garden. A sheet of blue tarpaulin covered most of it, so I couldn't be sure, but it seemed unlikely anyone would have a car-sized pile of rubbish behind their house with a sheet over it, unless they were trying to hide something.

'Is that what I think it is?' Carol's hand went to her mouth. 'Bloody hell, Terry.'

I held up a finger. 'Hang on, we need to be sure.' Pushing my way through to where the woods stopped, I stepped onto the grass. Nothing happened. No alarms went off, no-one leaped out at me brandishing a shotgun. I carried on towards the car. The lights from the house cast their glow over the course I was now on, but all I could do was hope no-one looked out the window.

Reaching the edge of the lawn, I stepped onto the gravel. The crunch was loud, but there was nothing I could do about that. Taking my time, I continued towards my objective, striving to keep the crunchiness to a minimum. Just as I reached it and had leaned forward to lift the edge of the tarpaulin, I heard another sound. Whirling round, I saw Carol poised with one foot in the air.

'I'm not staying there by myself,' she hissed. And in a sudden rush, she sprinted across to where I stood, kicking gravel everywhere. If there'd been anyone near the windows, they'd have heard the noise for sure.

Wasting no more time, I whipped the tarpaulin off the car. And there it was, the all-too familiar number plate attached to a red Nissan Crappy.

A sharp creak came from somewhere behind us. I looked at Carol. She looked at me. We turned around slowly.

'Well,' said Elise Andersson, 'It took you long enough.' She stepped back from the door and waved a hand. 'Come in for a moment. My husband would like to meet you.' She gave Carol a hard, impenetrable stare. 'You too, Ms Hutchinson.'

'Your husband?' I couldn't hide the apprehension in my voice. Maybe I'd been right all along about getting blown away, and this was when it was going to happen.

She must have read my thoughts. 'Don't worry, Terry, he won't kill you.' She laughed and walked back into the house.

I followed her in, having taken the precaution of picking up a handful of gravel and stuffing it into my coat pocket. I didn't imagine it'd be much use against an actual gun, but at least I'd feel there was still the possibility, however small, of defending myself and perhaps even staying alive.

The outside of the house was pretty shabby - the ancient sash windows looked as if they needed chucking out and replacing, and the back door was similarly disadvantaged. Inside, however, I was pleasantly surprised. The dark Victorian hovel I'd expected had been completely gutted, or at least was in the process of attaining guttedness. The stripped floorboards in the wide hallway that ran the length of the house to the front door, were varnished to a high standard and it looked like the staircase was in the process of getting the same treatment.

Elise was standing in the hall. She waited until Carol had closed the back door then she opened another door into what I guessed would be the kitchen. While the space beyond was definitely a place where food could be prepared, it had the look of one of those fancy open-plan restaurants that're all the rage these days. There was an Aga against one wall with a modern oven next to it. A massive traditional kitchen table commanded centre stage with a rack of pots and pans hanging overhead that the likes of Jamie Oliver wouldn't turn his nose up at.

A tall hunk of a man stood at the table, hunched over a silver machine. He appeared to be feeding raw meat into one end of it and disgorging lengths of condomed cock at the other end. He looked up as we entered and smiled at Elise.

'Guests? What a lovely surprise.' His voice was as unlike hers as a silk purse is to a pig's arse, but I had to admit even the Swedish accent couldn't disguise the rich tones of his vowels. I wouldn't have been surprised if he'd treated us to some traditional Swedish poetry, holding us enraptured with the beauty and majesty of his voice alone.

'Darling, say hello to Terry and Carol.' Elise turned and waved a hand as if we might be expected to perform some ritual dance.

'Hi.' It sounded lame in the context of the rich timbre of Sven's vocal talents, but it was the best I could do.

Carol squeaked a hello.

The blond hunk went back to his phallic pastime, but kept his gaze on us. 'Good to meet you at last, Terry. You like lamb?'

I coughed. 'Aye. I mean, yes, I like it fine.' If that was his way of inviting us to stay for dinner, it was a little too subtle. I decided to shut up and see what happened.

Elise slipped an arm around him and kissed his neck. 'My husband is the king of sausages, aren't you darling?'

I wondered if she was making saucy suggestions.

Thankfully, we didn't have to stand there watching Big Sven create his dick-sausages. Elise led us through to another room where a selection of leather sofas and low coffee tables suggested this was where they did their entertaining. She put on some music and I was surprised when it turned out to be Rachmaninoff's something or other in C minor. It wouldn't have been my choice of background music, but as it turned out, it fitted the bill rather well.

Carol and I perched on the edge of one of the sofas and I forced myself to concentrate while Elise poured drinks. She handed us each a glass of wine, then took another one through to the kitchen. When she returned, she leaned on the windowsill.

'Sven will be only a moment.' She smiled and picked up a magazine and started flicking through as if she were waiting for a dental appointment.

'Right.' I looked at Carol. This was beginning to feel like some sort of bizarre interview where our answers to their questions might have deadly repercussions.

'Still here, then?' The Swedish chef strolled in a few minutes later, sipping his wine. He crossed the room and turned the volume down a little on the hi-fi. He leaned against the cabinet, nestling his glass between his hands. 'Now, Terry. Carol.'

I coughed. Carol sniffed.

'Clearly, my dear wife did not invite you in so that we might entertain you.'

'No.' I coughed again, an irritating tickle at the back of my throat.

'You've been asking questions.'

I glanced at Elise. 'A bit more than that, actually.'

He smiled in a way that reminded me of Anthony Hopkins in Silence of the Lambs. I was glad we weren't drinking Chianti.

'Yes, you have, and while I may be prepared to overlook mere inquisitiveness, I would not wish you to dwell on a theory that is, shall we say, misguided.'

I decided to throw caution to the proverbials. 'Really? So you didn't kill Ronnie?' Carol let out gasp and grabbed my hand, but I'd started and I was going to finish. 'Cos from where we are it looks like you guys are running a brothel, providing sex slaves for your business cronies and knocking off anybody that gets in the way.' I glared at him. 'Is that about right?'

Sven took a sip of wine. 'A brothel, sex slaves, and yes, even the getting rid of those individuals who are in the way, yes. That is about right. However, in identifying myself and Elise as the ah...protagonists in this matter, you are most definitely wrong.' He glanced at Elise who was looking remarkably calm. 'Darling, I think perhaps our guests might not wish to stay for dinner after all.'

I moved my hand to where I'd stuffed the gravel into my pocket. Our Swedish friend didn't appear to be toting a gun, but that didn't mean he didn't have one stashed away nearby.

Sven sat on the sofa opposite and rubbed the bridge of his nose. 'Okay, let us be Frank.' He laughed softly. 'You see what I did there? Frank?' He laughed again. 'Tell me Mr Bell, what do think is the connection between your friend Frank and myself, or indeed, with Elise?'

I waved a hand at the window. 'His fuckin car's outside for a start.'

He nodded. 'Yes. Where he left it when he delivered a certain something to our house.'

'Really?' I became aware the tremor had come back into my voice and it wasn't going to go away.

He reached up and rubbed a hand over his head, then gazed at me with an expression that seemed caught between amusement and concern. When he spoke again, his voice was low and I found myself lulled into a strange sort of tranquillity. 'Frank and I met when he picked me up one night from the Hexagon. A few months ago now. I liked him, his attitude and his honesty were refreshing. He talked about his wife and her infidelities, his health problems and the lack of joy in his life. I thought we could help each other. So we came to an arrangement and he carried out a series of private jobs for us, which I know did not go through the books. Maybe that brought him into conflict with Ronnie.'

'Frank came here?' I said.

Sven nodded. 'Many times. He also helped us to infiltrate the set-up at Nugent Crescent, though only in a rather unsophisticated way. He accompanied Elise to several of Ahmed's parties in a bid to discover exactly what it was they were doing.'

'That doesn't explain why his car's in your back garden.'

Sven took a deep breath and let it out in a long slow sigh. 'Of course. You want proof. Very well.'

He looked at Elise. 'Would you mind?'

She seemed to consider this for a moment, then said, 'If you're sure?'

He nodded. 'I do not think our friends will leave until they are satisfied.'

Carol nudged me and gave me a you-okay? look. I gave her a quick nod.

Elise shook her head resignedly and went out. We heard her footsteps going up the stairs, shoes slapping the bare treads up to the top and along the landing. There was a short silence, then the slapping came back, this time accompanied by another set of footsteps.

I listened to the descending feet, trying to work out if the newcomer was male or female. When Elise came back into the room, a dark-skinned, slim woman followed her in. I looked up as they walked across to join Sven on the sofa.

When they'd sat down, Sven continued.

'This is Trudy. She speaks English, but not enough to explain the intricacies of her situation, therefore I will do the honours. Trudy lived with four other girls in a squat in Tynemouth while waitressing at the Hexagon. Elise and I dined there one particular evening when I'd asked Frank to pick us up. Trudy had served us during our meal. She had been attentive and charming, and as she was shortly to finish her shift, we offered to drop her off on our way home. Frank, being a gentleman, insisted on walking her to the door. The state of the flat appalled him. On the drive back here, he talked of nothing else, wanted to do something for her, to help her in some way. Unfortunately, Trudy had also been spotted by another customer at the Hexagon that night - Ronnie Thompson.' He half-smiled. 'Not a nice fellow.'

I shook my head and looked at Carol. She'd gone very pale.

Sven went on. 'It seems that Ronnie offered the girl a job waitressing at a party where Ahmed was one of the guests. Ahmed liked what he saw and handed over a large sum of money to Ronnie in exchange for delivering Trudy to Nugent Crescent, where she would be offered to one of their regular clients and then kept at some secret location as a sex slave.' His voice was matter of fact now, starkly unemotional. 'If Ronnie had done the job himself, we might never have heard of her again. His one mistake was to ask Frank to pick Trudy up and drive her to Nugent Crescent on the pretext of another waitressing job.'

'And that was last Friday?' I said.

He nodded solemnly. 'Frank was suspicious, but drove her to the house as planned. Leaving Trudy in the car, he spoke to one of Ahmed's henchmen who pointed out the client she was to spend the night with. Frank realised what was going on and, pretending to fetch the girl, drove her to his own house instead. Of course, he knew by taking her there he'd simply placed them both in danger. These people are not the kind to throw money away.'

'Frank wasn't stupid,' I said. 'He'd have gone to

the police.'

'As you say, he wasn't stupid, which is why he did *not* go to the police.' He turned and smiled at Trudy. She smiled back. 'You see,' he went on, 'Trudy is an illegal immigrant. Frank knew this. He also knew she could suffer considerable abuse, even death, if she were forced to return to her own country.' He shrugged. 'So he brought her here.'

For a moment, I didn't know what to say. It all sounded plausible, though there were still plenty of unanswered questions. Eventually, I said, 'Go on.'

He nodded and took a sip of wine. 'He turned up about eleven o'clock that night in a state of great anxiety. By the time he'd told us what he'd done, the stress of it all became too much and he suffered a massive heart attack. He was dead before he hit the floor.'

Sven leaned forward, his face creased up, and for the first time, I saw something approaching sorrow take hold of his features. 'There was nothing we could do. Even if there had been, we could not have brought ambulances and doctors here since that would prompt questions, which in turn would necessitate the truth of Trudy's situation being made public, and that is something we could not allow to happen. So Elise and I made a decision. Perhaps it was not the right one, but we made it all the same. We drove to Frank's house in his car, placed his body on the table and made him as comfortable as possible. Then we came home and did our best to erase all links to Trudy that might lead anyone to this house in search of her.'

The five of us sat in silence for a long moment, then Carol leaned forward. 'Sorry, I'm confused. Who killed Ronnie?'

Sven looked at me and raised an eyebrow. 'Perhaps you would like to continue, Terry? I'm sure you have your own theories?'

'Right.' I took a breath. 'Ronnie came looking for me because he thought Frank might have told me about Trudy.' I glanced at Sven and he nodded. 'Which he had, as it happens, just not the entire truth.' I hesitated, getting my thoughts in order. 'Ahmed, or Ahmed's men must have been watching Ronnie and they thought, I dunno, he'd double-crossed them. And presumably Ahmed also thought we knew where Trudy was.'

Sven nodded again. 'That is the most likely explanation, though I doubt if Mr Ahmed will ever confess to such a thing.'

'So,' put in Carol, 'it was Ahmed's lot that torched our caravan and broke into the flat and left the notes?'

'I know nothing of any notes or break-ins but, yes, I would say so.'

It made sense, but there were a couple of things that didn't sit right. 'What about Ralph? I know he came here cos I brought him here. So he knows you.'

Sven allowed himself a smile. 'Ah, yes. But again, I suspect you already know the answer yourself?'

I stared at him.

He nodded. 'Think about it.'

I cast my mind back to how I'd first met Ralph, how I'd thought he was the man called Horse at Nugent Crescent and that he knew Elise and... I nodded. Of course. 'He works for you.'

'For me and for Mrs Carver, though please don't tell her I told you. Also, you would do well not to berate him for not being completely honest. After all, you might not be here if it were not for his actions.'

I sat back and looked at him. 'Why's Frank's car here?'

'Our own car would be more likely to be remembered, so we drove the Nissan to Frank's house and then back here.' He made a vague gesture. 'Sometimes more rational choices are obvious only in retrospect. At the time, we thought it might give us an advantage if the car was missing. In any case, after his body had been found, we could hardly put it back, could we?' He shrugged.

'I suppose not,' I said. My head was buzzing with all this new information. I tried to focus on the things I still didn't know. 'What about the industrial unit where me and Ralph were locked up? That was one of yours.'

He shook his head. 'We run a security firm which monitors a number of units for several clients, one of which is Sanjay Ahmed. It was his property you were confined in, not ours.'

Carol waved a hand. 'Hang on, you're sayin you and Ahmed are mates?'

Again, he shook his head. 'We had legitimate dealings with his construction supply company and that would have continued had we not suspected there was something more sinister going on. We had taken part in a handful of planning meetings believing Ahmed intended offering us a partnership. However, some of the other individuals at one of those meetings were quite obviously not interested in construction.' He glanced at Elise. 'My wife is something of an amateur sleuth, which is why she accepted invitations to a number of parties in an effort to learn the truth. Frank was her driver and acted as a party guest in a bid to discover where the women were being held, if indeed, there were any women. Ralph monitored things from a house across the street, but we had no idea there was a second house. In that respect, it seems you aided us to the winning post.' He smiled.

'And David? He says you paid him to scare us off.'

His face creased in a frown and he shook his head sadly. 'I suspect David will say what he has to in order to avoid blame. When Frank took Trudy to Nugent Crescent, he discovered she'd been chosen for a specific client, one who has a penchant for a particular type of sexual abuse. That client was your brother-in-law, David Seaton.'

Chapter 18

Frank's funeral was the following Friday, exactly two weeks after his death. Lizzy was there of course, but apart from passing on my condolences, I kept out of her way. She'd already put the house up for sale and moved in with Dave from the arcade, but to be honest, I didn't care any more. The important thing was that Frank had found some happiness before he died, albeit briefly.

It felt like there were still a lot of loose ends to tie up, niggling things didn't make sense - like who had texted me from Ronnie's phone, and which of my taxi-driver mates had been dropping hints to Ahmed. And I was pretty sure Sven hadn't told me the whole truth either, but as the police didn't have much to say about it, there wasn't much point pursuing the matter.

On the Ronnie front, I wasn't convinced Ken was innocent in the whole affair, but given that his wife and his son were dead, it didn't seem right to punish him any more, especially since I didn't actually know he'd done anything wrong. He also finally got around to paying me for the outstanding fares on the Sangster account and while he was in the mood for handing out cash, I suggested he give Carol a pay rise, which he did. He never mentioned the ten grand Frank owed Ronnie.

Though I didn't get my phone or my wallet back,

Mrs Carver sent round a Harrods hamper full of lovely grub, as well as a neat bundle of fifty-pound notes. The money paid for new lava lamps and some vintage travel posters, as well as a CD of that Rachmaninoff thing in C minor.

Charis rang me for what she called a 'friendly chat', but when it came down to it, she didn't have much to say. I got the impression she was fishing for something on a personal level, but as far as that was concerned, I wasn't biting. However, she did confirm that David was still 'helping with enquiries' and that our Jessie had been arrested for 'assault with an empty bottle of Pinot Grigio', but apart from that it was a bit of a one-horse conversation.

A few days after the funeral, when things had settled down and I'd agreed to do three days a week to help Ken out on the taxis, I pulled off the rank one morning to do a pickup from a phone box on the Esplanade. I was surprised to see Ralph leaning against the sea wall.

'Thought I'd give yer a bit of time to get used to the idea,' he said, sliding in beside me.

'What idea's that, Ralph?'

'Oh you know, me not tellin you everything.'

'Aye, well, I found out in the end, didn't I?'

'Aye.'

'So d'you want to go anywhere or is this just a sit-and-wait?'

'Just a sit-and-wait.' He grinned. 'Might have a job for you, though.'

I shook my head. 'Not workin with you again, ye

lying fucker.'

He laughed. 'You will though. But maybe not just yet, eh?' He punched me on the shoulder and climbed out the car. 'See ye round.'

I watched him walk across the road and climb into a black Volvo with tinted windows. It was a new one. He'd obviously done something to deserve it.

###

Author's Note

Quarter of a century ago, I spent a bit of time driving a taxi in a nice, quiet seaside town on the east coast. I got to drive a new car, swan around during the summer months in shirt-sleeves and sunglasses and pick up a lot of young women. Trouble is, I also picked up drunks, pimps, villains and the occasional prostitute. It wasn't a glamorous lifestyle and I soon tired of it, but I saw a side to the town that intrigued me, so it was only a matter of time before the place made its way into one of my books.

Having said that, when I did start writing about it, the seaside town that kept popping into my imagination was one much nearer home - on the northeast coast near Newcastle. Consequently, Terry Bell's stomping ground is a kind of fictitious mix of people and places, and while he does turn up in a few real-life locations, most of those mentioned in the town itself don't exist.

Writing, as they say, is a solitary business and being an indie author is no different. However, indie authors are a supportive lot and I've been lucky in forging some great friendships among the online writing community over the last couple of years, as well as gaining a lot of useful tips and ideas about the technical and marketing sides of self-publishing.

I'd like to say a big thank you to everyone on my Facebook Launch Team and to all my pals in the *OSFARG* and *Book Connectors* groups who've always been supportive and encouraging. Particular thanks go to my heroes Kathryn Bax, Shaun Griffiths and Diana Febry, who are regularly on hand with advice and common sense - you guys have helped me (and many others) keep the newbie mistakes to a minimum. In addition, thanks to Joy Mutter for pointing out the mistakes that should have been obvious, as well as the ones I'd never have noticed if I'd tripped over them in the street.

As a postscript to the original version of 'Death on a Dirty Afternoon', I'd like to say a special thank you to Glynis Laidlaw for her editing skills and for reminding me that my knowledge of punctuation still has room to grow.

Colin Garrow
August 2017

Excerpt from 'A Long Cool Glass of Murder'
Book 2 in the 'Terry Bell Mysteries'

Chapter 1

I knew as soon as I reached the top of the stairs that something was wrong. Tina Overton wasn't the sort of woman to go around leaving her front door open, neither was she the sort whose tastes included screechy violin music. The final bars of something discordant and unappealing in a fingernails-scraping-down-a-blackboard sort of way, floated out from somewhere beyond the open doorway, heading for an equally unappealing climax.

But that wasn't the problem. The problem was the bad feeling in my gut. The one that had been foisting itself on me at regular intervals ever since the last time I'd discovered a dead body. I consoled myself with the observation that at least this time it would be occupying someone else's living room floor, rather than mine.

Even so, the thought that it might be happening again gave me the jitters.

And it was stupid. I knew it was. Such calamities happen once in a lifetime, like crashing your car into a petrol tanker and bursting into flames, falling out of a fourteenth-storey window and landing on the pavement like a lump of strawberry jam, or getting struck by lightning. And as everyone knows, strawberry jam doesn't strike twice.

I stared at the door. Listened to the screechy music.

If this were a horror movie starring yours truly as the poor fool who gets decapitated in the first scene, I'd naturally push the door open and incline my head at an appropriate angle for the benefit of the knife-wielding madman waiting on the other side. The camera would switch to the suitably sharpened machete slicing through the air towards the victim's neck two seconds after he's opened his mouth to scream. But this wasn't a movie, and if it had been, I'm not the sort of bloke who'd stand around waiting for the first cut, deep or otherwise. No, I'd be off down the stairs like a bat in a shitstorm.

I told myself to get a grip and stop being a wimp. There was no psycho-killer on the loose, just a part-time taxi driver keeping an appointment with a woman who thinks her husband's trying to kill her.

Yes. It was all perfectly normal.

I knocked on the door. "Tina?"

No answer.

The door had moved a smidgen inwards at my knock. I leaned forward but all I could see was the passageway that led to her living room and kitchen. A line from a novel popped into my head - something about blood on the carpet and murder in the hall. It wasn't an image I wanted to cultivate.

Pushing the thought away, I tried to concentrate on realistic possibilities. Tina had probably nipped to the lavvy or gone out on the fire escape to have a quiet smoke. Except, if she was having a smoke, then the fire door would be open creating a through-draught that'd cause the currently half-open front door to slam shut.

Okay, scrap that one and go with the toilet scenario - after all, that's the most likely. Any minute now she'll appear in the hallway apologising for not hearing the door and asking if I'd like a coffee. Then we'd settle down to discuss whatever it was she'd asked me over here to talk about.

Then the music stopped.

I listened, moved a tad nearer the door, but there was nothing else to hear - none of the familiar sounds of everyday life, normality, human existence.

Giving the door a push, I called out a feeble, "Tina? Ye there, pet?"

Still no answer.

A door slammed downstairs and I remembered that the communal entrance had also been open. Course, that's nothing unusual in flats like these. Stepping across the landing, I peered into the darkness below. The stairwell was empty, unless whoever had made the noise was lurking in the shadows. I was starting to wish I'd come over earlier when it was still daylight.

Looking back at the still-open door, I decided it was time to quit conjuring up nightmare scenarios and just go inside. At worst, Tina might be a bit miffed at my having simply strolled in unannounced, but at least I'd find out if she was actually there.

I could smell it before I was half-way along the passage. I'd been in the flat only once before and on that occasion I'd got as far as the kitchen. We shared a love of freshly ground coffee and I reckoned Tina had put one on especially for me.

"Tina?"

Of the seven doors that opened off the passage, I knew which one led to the kitchen, but otherwise I was lost.

As I stood there contemplating my next move, something changed. At first I wasn't sure what it was, then I realised the music has started up again. It was one of those annoying compositions that begin so quietly you're not sure if it's actually started yet, before rising to an ear-splitting crescendo after about half an hour. Not being over acquainted with classical music, and only having one such piece in my possession, I knew it wasn't Rachmaninov.

The one thing I did know was that the music was coming from the door nearest me. I grasped the brass knob and gave it a twist. Immediately, the orchestra's efforts increased in volume. Pushing the door open, I peeked inside.

The first thing I saw was the metal tea tray leaning against the side of the sofa, then as my eyes slid across the floor, I took in the reel-to-reel tape player on the coffee table, its yellowing spools turning slowly. I kept my eyes fixed on the machine for a few long seconds, like a rabbit in the headlights, aware that my peripheral vision was telling me Tina Overton was close at hand, waiting for my consideration.

I'd have been happy not to look, to simply keep my head down and retreat from the scene, content in the knowledge that sooner or later someone else would discover whatever mischief had been done here. But the lure of the grotesque was irresistible. I raised my head and gradually swivelled my eyes towards the woman on the sofa. And there she was, slouched down, a mug of coffee on the small table at her side.

If her mouth hadn't been open, maybe I'd have been spared the whitish foam that had dribbled down the side of her face. But it was her eyes that gave that game away - they were wide and staring, gazing at the far wall, as if some unseen object had caught her attention in the moment of her death.

I was glad that at least she didn't have her face bashed in like Big Ronnie, but in a grotesque sort of way, that might have been less offensive than the pale, rather surprised look on her features.

It was while I was stood there wondering what the hell to do next, that I heard the unmistakable creak of floorboards. I remembered the slamming of the main door, the absence of a neighbour's footsteps clomping up the stairs, the lack of anything remotely normal since I'd stepped into the communal entrance hall.

There was another creak. I started to turn round and in doing so, my foot kicked the tea tray, knocking it over with a clatter that would've woken Tina Overton, if she hadn't been dead.

I looked down at the tray and as soon as I did, I knew whoever was in the hallway had stepped into the room.

"Oh Christ, you've got to be fucking joking?"

Charis Brown's elfin-like smile was, like the footsteps on the stairs, noticeably absent. She looked at me, looked at the dead woman, and let out the sort of sigh I knew from experience meant it was going to be a long night.

###

Thank you for taking the time to read 'Death on a Dirty Afternoon.' If you enjoyed it, please consider telling your friends or posting a short review. Word of mouth is an author's best friend and much appreciated.

Sincerely,
Colin Garrow

Other Books by this Author

Books for Adults

Death on a Dirty Afternoon
A Long Cool Glass of Murder
The Jansson Tapes
Six Feet Under
Blood on the Tyne: Body Parts
Blood on the Tyne: Head Shots
Terminal Black
The Watson Letters Vol 1: Something Wicker This Way Comes
The Watson Letters Vol 2: Not the 39 Steps
The Watson Letters Vol 3: Curse of the Baskervilles
The Watson Letters Vol 4: Revenge of the Hooded Claw
The Watson Letters Vol 5: Murder on Mystery Island

Story Collections

How the World Turns (and Other Stories)
Girlfriend, Interrupted

Stage Plays

Love Song in Sixteen Bars
Towards the Inevitability of Catastrophe
The Body in the Bag

Non-Fiction

Writing: Ideas and Inspirations (or How to Make Things Up)

Books for Children

The Demon of Devilgate Drive
The Curse of Callico Jack
The Architect's Apprentice
Mortlake
The Devil's Porridge Gang
The Hounds of Hellerby Hall
The House That Wasn't There

Connect with Me

(All Feedback Welcome)
mailto: hello@colingarrow.org

Websites:
http://colingarrow.org
https://thewatsonletters.com
https://colingarrowbooks.com

Twitter:
https://twitter.com/colingarrow

Facebook: https://www.facebook.com/colingarrowthewriter

Amazon Author Page:
http://www.amazon.com/ColinGarrow/e/B014Z5DZD4

The Watson Letters Blog:
https://thewatsonletters.wordpress.com/

About the Author

Colin Garrow grew up in a former mining town in Northumberland. He has worked in a plethora of professions including: taxi driver, antiques dealer, drama facilitator, theatre director and fish processor, and has occasionally masqueraded as a pirate.

All Colin's books are available as eBooks and most are also out in paperback. His short stories have appeared in several literary mags, including: SN Review, Flash Fiction Magazine, Word Bohemia, Every Day Fiction, The Grind, A3 Review, 1,000 Words, Inkapture and Scribble Magazine.

He currently lives in a humble cottage in North East Scotland where he writes novels, stories, poems and the occasional song.

Printed in Great Britain
by Amazon